"I'm Amazed You Came Here Alone Tonight."

His hand came out of nowhere to cup her chin. "What's to stop me from sharpening my fangs on your lovely throat?" She tried to rise, but his hand on her shoulder prevented her. "Don't run now, Dany."

"Stop it. You're trying to frighten me."

"So what if I frighten you a little? There's a curious pleasure in it, wouldn't you agree? There's an exciting rush in the heightened awareness, the pounding of the blood, the racing of the mind that you feel when you're afraid."

Dany felt the rush. She shut her eyes to escape his mesmerizing stare. *Vampires can fix their victims with their gaze, rendering them helpless.* "You're so tempting," he whispered, lowering his head until she felt that demonic mouth hovering over her neck....

Dear Reader:

Series and Spin-offs! Connecting characters and intriguing interconnections to make your head whirl.

In Joan Hohl's successful trilogy for Silhouette Desire—*Texas Gold* (7/86), *California Copper* (10/86), *Nevada Silver* (1/87)—Joan created a cast of characters that just wouldn't quit. You figure out how *Lady Ice* (5/87) connects. And in August, "J.B." demanded his own story—*One Tough Hombre*. In *Falcon's Flight*, coming in November, you'll learn *all* about . . .?

Annette Broadrick's *Return to Yesterday* (6/87) introduced Adam St. Clair. This August *Adam's Story* tells about the woman who saves his life—and teaches him a thing or two about love!

The six Branigan brothers appeared in Leslie Davis Guccione's *Bittersweet Harvest* (10/86) and *Still Waters* (5/87). September brings *Something in Common*, where the eldest of the strapping Irishmen finds love in unexpected places.

Midnight Rambler by Linda Barlow is in October—a special Halloween surprise, and totally unconnected to anything.

Keep an eye out for other Silhouette Desire favorites—Diana Palmer, Dixie Browning, Ann Major and Elizabeth Lowell, to name a few. You never know when secondary characters will insist on their own story. . . .

All the best,

Isabel Swift
Senior Editor & Editorial Coordinator
Silhouette Books

LINDA BARLOW
Midnight Rambler

Silhouette Desire

Published by Silhouette Books New York

America's Publisher of Contemporary Romance

SILHOUETTE BOOKS
300 East 42nd St., New York, N.Y. 10017

Copyright © 1987 by Linda Barlow

ISBN: 0-373-05379-7

First Silhouette Books printing October 1987

America's Publisher of Contemporary Romance

Printed in the U.S.A.

LINDA BARLOW

writes in several fields, including historical romance, mainstream fiction and contemporary romance. She's been daydreaming for years about "strong, tender heroes with a piratical gleam in their eyes" and believes she may have known a few of them in her various former lives. Linda lives with her husband and daughter outside Boston where she spends most her time reading, writing, riding her bike and running up huge phone bills.

To Louis and Lestat,
who inspired me

One

"There's no such thing as vampires."

Dany Holland repeated this statement several times as she guided her rickety Toyota up the slick mountain road outside of Chesterton, New Hampshire. She drove slowly, keeping a lookout for the private driveway that would lead to Max Rambler's house, a building that was something of a Gothic monstrosity, if rumor were to be believed. "A castle, complete with dungeons and chains," Casper Pearson, her administrative assistant at St. Crispin's School had told her. He'd then gleefully gone on to describe its owner as "a real weirdo, a recluse and a mad genius of high technology."

"He must be very bizarre if *you* think he's weird," Dany had replied. Cass, who dressed in leather and sported a punk haircut, was hardly the epitome of normal.

"I've never met him," Pearson had admitted. "Don't know many people who have."

Dany knew one. David Ellis, one of her students, had even stranger things to report of Mr. Max Rambler. According to David, Rambler was a vampire.

Dany's head ached slightly at the thought. A vampire. She had not become headmistress of the formidable and very proper St. Crispin's School at the age of thirty by believing in such nonsense.

Still, Dany wished that Rambler, an eccentric computer inventor of considerable renown, had agreed to meet with her during the day instead of after sunset. And she wished he hadn't sounded so sinister on the phone when he'd informed her, "I'm a night person, Ms. Holland. I sleep during the day."

"In your coffin, I suppose?"

He hadn't denied it. He'd just laughed.

Rounding a bend in the road, she saw a decrepit sign on which she could barely make out the word *Rambler*. She applied the brakes and turned left. The next leg of her journey involved negotiating a dirt road set into the lee of what seemed to be the steepest section of Glencrag, one of the foothills of New Hampshire's White Mountains. The road was slippery, and she cursed as she skidded. The lacy branches overhead were still dripping with the afternoon's rain. Although the sky had cleared within the last hour or so, the temperature had dipped, turning puddles into something perilously close to ice.

"Damn," she muttered, gripping the wheel more tightly. One thing Dany didn't like about her job was the driving on hilly roads that were snow-covered for so many months of the year. This was only October; imagine what February would be like. Compared to La Jolla, California, Chesterton was as inhospitable as the North Pole.

"Don't be such a wimp," she muttered to herself. She'd grown up in New Hampshire, after all, and her roots were here. After Greg had abandoned her and Sarah in California, making it clear he had no intention of ever coming back, Dany had decided to return to her home state so her daughter could be near her grandparents. She'd been hired last spring to replace St. Crispin's former headmistress, Edith Kenworthy, the crusty educator who had died suddenly after directing the course of the private school for three decades. Although Dany didn't agree in all particulars with her predecessor's educational philosophy, she was a single mother now, and she'd been thankful to get the job.

"Now all you have to do is keep it," she wryly reminded herself. Which meant rousting out all threats to her authority, including any pesky creatures of the night.

After climbing far higher than she cared to on such a treacherous road, Dany turned left and emerged into a small clearing. She looked in vain for some sign of a house, but there were no lights anywhere. Overhead she could see a bright blanket of stars and, just rising from the treetops, the silver crescent of the new moon. The rain had ended, leaving behind a clear, sparkling night. But it was very dark.

She drove on a little farther, following a gravel driveway, which she assumed would lead to Rambler's house. When at last the headlights fixed upon the building looming up before her, Dany was ashamed to catch herself contemplating a quick retreat. With its high gabled roof, gargoyled entryway and tall, staring windows through which no trace of light gleamed, the place could have served as a set for a Dracula movie.

"I'm telling you, Ms. Holland, the guy's a vampire," David had told her yesterday in her office at St. Crispin's. He'd come to her with an incredible tale. She'd heard some winners during her career as a high-school English teacher and assistant principal; after all, teenagers tended to be highly imaginative. But this topped everything.

"David, that's impossible. Vampires are mythical figures. They don't exist."

"That's what they want us mortals to think. That's why they're so powerful, so dangerous. They wander among us, safely stalking their victims as they hide behind the comfortable veil of myth."

"Nonsense."

"Haven't you ever played Hunt the Night City? Max Rambler created it. It's a classic board game, Ms. Holland. And everything it tells us about vampires is true!"

"I thought Mr. Rambler was a computer genius, not a creator of board games."

"He is. But the greatest thing he ever created was the game."

Absently, Dany fingered a loose tendril of her red-gold hair as she considered the boy. Like her, David was relatively new to St. Crispin's. He'd transferred to the school last semester from somewhere out west. Because he'd participated in a fund-raising drama club production that had been slapped together only a week ago with Dany's help, she knew him better than she knew most of his fellow students. He was shy but bright. He had already carved out a niche for himself as a character actor in the drama club, and his grades were excellent, particularly in science and math. He would graduate with highest honors next year…if he didn't rush off to join the ranks of the undead.

"Max Rambler is a well-known scientist, who has invented various computer-related hardware," said Dany. "He's rather eccentric, I understand, but he's certainly not a vampire."

David shifted uneasily, saying nothing.

"Why don't you talk to me about what's really bothering you?" she'd added more gently. "Are you having some problems with your studies? With your friends? With a girlfriend, perhaps?"

St. Crispin's students were not supposed to have girlfriends or boyfriends. Dating was against the former headmistress's stringent regulations. But Dany suspected it was a rule more honored in the breach than in the observance.

If so, David would not admit it. "My problems," he said repressively, "are with vampires."

Exasperated, Dany rose to her feet. "You're obviously having some sort of joke with me. I'm not lacking in humor, but I really can't allow my time to be wasted in this manner, David."

When David realized he was about to be dismissed, his demeanor changed so abruptly that Dany regretted her sharp words. His expression seemed to crumple; he looked scared. "I'm not kidding, Ms. Holland. If you don't believe me, I'll just have to prove it to you. Look."

David ripped off his tie and pulled at the collar of his shirt. The formal attire was odd, Dany acknowledged belatedly. Most of the kids went around in loud T-shirts and rumpled sports jackets, emulating the sartorial splendor of the cops on a popular television show.

After unbuttoning the top two buttons of his shirt, David jerked it to the side. There, just at the point where his throat met his shoulder, was a bluish bruise. "He attacked me. He tried to suck my blood, but someone came by so he ran off." He shuddered. "Don't you see? I'm lucky to be alive."

"My God!" Dany stared at the mark. It had two darker points at the center that David insisted had been caused by the vampire's fangs. Absurd! Yet she couldn't control the atavistic shiver that ran through her skeptical twentieth-century limbs.

Deep inside her ran a persistent streak of superstition. She supposed there were lots of people who shared her aversion to broken mirrors and black cats; people who, like Dany, sneaked a look at their horoscopes before getting on an airplane, just to make sure there was no warning not to travel that day. Everything she'd read on the subject assured her that such foolishness ran rampant, even in the rational, scientific U.S.A.

Like many people, Dany loved to scare herself silly now and then with a juicy Gothic tale or a well-made horror movie, but actually to believe in vampires? That, surely, was carrying superstition a little too far.

"David, are you seriously telling me that Max Rambler crept up on you at night and sank his teeth into your throat?"

"Well, it was dark and I didn't get a good look at his face. But he was tall and thin, like Rambler. And he was wearing this huge gold ring that Rambler wears. I caught a glimpse of his hand as he grabbed me. He had awesome long fingers with shiny nails."

"Have you ever met Mr. Rambler?"

"Yeah, I have. He gave a lecture in Chesterton last spring on artificial intelligence. You know, robots and stuff? I talked to him briefly afterward. About Hunt the Night City, which I had just started playing at the time. He seemed interested in me—asked me a lot of questions about myself. The other night, when he attacked me, he said my name, and I recognized his voice."

It was at this point that Dany began to take David seriously. Not that she thought the bruise was really the mark of a vampire. But it was possible that Max Rambler was some kind of nut who took pleasure in frightening the kids at St. Crispin's. She'd heard he was a recluse, somewhat peculiar in his habits. Maybe he was more peculiar than anybody had realized.

Whatever the explanation might be, Dany was determined to get to the bottom of it. Quickly, before any more of her students were frightened. "Tell me more about this game, David. How exactly do you play it?"

David explained that the original board game had been superseded by a dramatized version in which students acted out the various roles. Some kids pretended to be vampires and others took the part of humans. If you were human, you had to do everything in your power to avoid being captured and subjected to the deadly vampire kiss. If you were a vampire, you had to take an occasional victim or risk dying of starvation.

"There are master vampires and slave vampires. And above them all is the Ancient One, the master of them all. No one knows who he is. Some say he's a real vampire, Ms. Holland. Some say he's Max Rambler himself."

"Who says? Has anyone else besides you identified him?"

He shrugged. "I'm not sure."

Another question occurred to her. "When the kids pretending to be vampires 'kill' their victims, do they really suck their necks?"

"No. They tap you on the shoulder, that's all. I mean, nobody ever gets hurt, or anything." He touched his collar ruefully. "Not usually, anyway. It's just a game."

But it reminded Dany of some of the other medieval dungeon fantasy games she'd heard about kids playing at other schools and colleges. To most players, yes, it was "just a game." To someone who was emotionally weak or disturbed, an aggressive fantasy of this type could occasionally cause real psychological distress.

Dany tried to conceal from David her dismay that Hunt the Night City was being played at St. Crispin's. When she'd been offered the job, the trustees had seemed to rule out the possibility of any such goings-on. "This is a well-disciplined establishment," one of them had told her. "Parents send their children here because Mrs. Kenworthy refused to tolerate the outrageous and immoral behavior that takes place in the public schools."

Dany tried to imagine explaining vampire fantasy games to these demanding parents. Or to the conservative trustees who had hired her. Her head began to throb at the thought.

"The rumor is that one day soon the Ancient One will take a real victim," David added.

Dany swallowed. This is *nonsense*, she thought. "Kill someone, you mean?"

"Yes." David hugged himself, his eyes wide and dark. "That's what they say."

The boy was obviously scared, and it was because of this that Dany had braved a slick mountain road to have a talk with the reclusive technologist and alleged vampire, Max Rambler. It infuriated her to think that a grown man might be going around terrorizing teenagers. If Rambler was indeed the guilty party, she intended to make it clear to him that he'd better find some other arena for his kinky pranks.

Still, as she stared up at the ancient structure that Rambler called home, Dany couldn't help wishing the place weren't so isolated and the night so dark. Her superstitious streak was certainly making itself felt. As she parked the Toyota and sallied forth, a little voice inside her whispered that she should have brought a crucifix or some garlic with her, just in case. You've been reading too many occult novels, she said to herself. Max Rambler's just a man, and nothing more.

The click of Dany's heels on the stone steps that led to the massive front door sounded appallingly loud to her. The night was otherwise so silent, as if holding its breath for her passing.

She rang the ornate wrought-iron doorbell and heard somber chimes echoing inside. Then nothing. No lights, no movement, no sound. She frowned at the stone demon giving out a silent roar from a fresco over the door. It had the body of a lion and the head of a falcon. Good Lord, the thing looked as if it were contemplating coming alive and swallowing her. Squaring her shoulders, she stuck her tongue out at the beast.

She rang again. Maybe the master wasn't at home. Maybe she'd driven all the way up here for nothing. Maybe he'd forgotten the appointment and gone out to frighten a few students. Not only was he an eccentric, he was rude, as well.

She was so busy condemning Max Rambler's discourtesy—while at the same time secretly thanking heaven for it—that when the huge door opened inward a crack she involuntarily retreated a step or two. With a metallic shudder, the door opened the rest of the way. A shadowy figure was standing on the threshold, holding a silver candelabrum. The candlelight obscured rather than delineated his features, but Dany could see that he was slender and tall, as David had indicated.

"Mr. Rambler? I'm Danielle Holland."

Silence. The phantom raised the candelabrum higher. Nervously, Dany pushed an undisciplined lock of hair out of her eyes. Her long wavy hair never stayed for long in the chignons she forced it into, much to her annoyance. But it occurred to her now that she shouldn't have attempted the chignon tonight—it needlessly exposed her throat!

"We had an appointment tonight," she went on doggedly. "I'm sorry if I'm a few minutes late, but the road was treacherous and I had to drive slowly."

He stared at her. For some reason he made her feel small, although she was slightly over five foot seven. She tilted her chin, squinting as she tried to see him through the blaze of the candles. She received an impression of someone who was graceful yet strong.

"Is there something wrong?" she asked. "Surely you're not afraid to let me in?"

Once again she heard the laugh she remembered from their brief telephone conversation. It was low and husky, really quite pleasant. "No, I'm not afraid to let you in, if you're brave enough to enter."

"Is there something about you I ought to fear, Mr. Rambler?" Her tone implied that the idea was absurd.

Again the soft laugh. "No, of course not. Although if there were, you surely wouldn't expect me to admit it."

He threw the heavy door open wide, bowed and made her a flourish. The candlelight illuminated him now. Dany tried not to stare. For some reason she hadn't expected a computer buff to be so startlingly handsome.

The first thing she noticed was his luminous green eyes, through which all the wisdom of the ages seemed to shine. His thick, charcoal-black hair was cut slightly longer than was currently fashionable, framing a sensitive face marked by high cheekbones, an autocratic nose and a full, sensual mouth. The mouth transfixed her for a moment. It was decidedly erotic.

Don't even think such a thing, Dany. You came here to give him a piece of your mind, not to swoon over his sexy good looks.

His age was indeterminate. Although Cass Pearson had declared Rambler to be in his mid-thirties, he appeared younger. There was no gray in his hair, and except for a few laugh lines around his eyes, his face was smooth and unmarked. Even so, something about him conveyed a subtle air of competence and maturity.

He was not, she was relieved to see, wearing a black tux and a cape. Instead his long, angular limbs were conventionally clad in a tight pair of jeans and a ragged black sweater.

"Well? In or out, Ms. Holland? I'm afraid it's up to you either to run or take the plunge."

"Really, Mr. Rambler."

Drawing a deep but hopefully inaudible breath, Dany stepped into the house. Max Rambler closed the door behind her with a final-sounding click.

"Welcome to my lair, Headmistress," he said.

Two

Your lair?'' she repeated dryly. At least she hoped her tone was dry. Her mouth certainly was. She looked around, able to see no more than a few feet into the impenetrable gloom. ''Mausoleum might be a better term for it. Don't you have any electricity?''

Max Rambler was leaning back against the door now, holding the candles high and studying her with as much interest as she had been studying him. She felt those gleaming jade eyes moving over her with an intimacy that was disturbing. Nervously she touched her hand to her throat, then quickly took it away when his gaze followed. Don't encourage him, Dany! she said to herself.

''I'm in the process of having the place rewired. The house is ninety years old. The original wiring was a fire hazard.''

Vampires don't like bright lights. Last night, after her talk with David, Dany had dug through her library of horror fiction, searching out information on vampires. She didn't have as many books on the subject as she'd hoped; vampires had never been one of her favorite Gothic turn-ons. She preferred ghosts.

She'd stayed up late, familiarizing herself with the traits and habits of the undead. Pure fantasy, of course. Vampires preferred candlelight, although they had unusually acute sensory powers and could move around freely in pitch-darkness. The sun was anathema to them. It had the power to burn and destroy them, which was why they spent the daylight hours locked in their coffins.

"Let's go into my study," Rambler said. "I do have electricity in there. Follow me, okay? Watch out for the cat."

He took a few steps, then stopped so abruptly that she nearly ran into him. "You're not allergic to cats, are you?"

"No. I like cats."

But she was glad he'd warned her, for the cat, which she hadn't even seen, chose that moment to rub up against her and begin purring like a freight train. "Seems like an affable cat. What's its name?"

Max bent down and lifted the beast into his arms. It was a monstrous animal with mustard-yellow eyes. "Joe."

"Joe?" The name reassured her immensely. She'd expected the cat to be named Satan or Lestat.

"Short for the biblical Joseph with the coat of many colors. He's got black, brown, gray and white mixed in his fur."

That was even better. Vampires didn't read the Bible, did they? "I'm surprised you can even see his colors in this gloom."

"It's better in here."

He led her down a musty-smelling corridor that reminded her of a medieval gallery. Candlelight dimly illuminated several faded tapestries on the walls. At the end of the hall he ushered her into a square room lined like a library with wall-to-wall books. The floor was covered with faded Oriental carpets, and a fire was burning on the hearth. There was some recessed lighting near the ceiling, and a small fluorescent desk lamp cast a bright circle on a sheaf of papers on an open rolltop desk. Beside the desk were two long tables equipped with the latest in sophisticated computer paraphernalia: consoles, modems, screens, tape drives, disk drives and at least two printers. One of the screens was glowing amber.

"Am I taking you away from your work?" she asked.

"Don't worry about it. I've been struggling through a very uncreative period lately anyway."

He waved her toward a ponderous maroon sofa that stood opposite the fire. It was clearly an antique. With the exception of the computers, all the furnishings in the room were antiques. "Have a seat, Ms. Holland. Can I get you something?" He turned to what appeared to be an amply stocked bar. "Cognac, perhaps?"

"Sure, if you join me."

"No thanks. I don't drink."

Vampires don't eat or drink. They subsist entirely on the blood of their victims.

"Puts me right to sleep," he added with a disarming smile. "I'm hoping to get some work done after you leave tonight."

He poured cognac into a delicate crystal glass and handed it to her. She accepted it, noting that he was wearing a heavy gold ring on his right hand, just as David had described. His hands were elegant, with long, narrow fingers. Yet they also looked punishingly strong. His nails gleamed as if he'd polished them—hadn't David mentioned something about that? She tried to drown her nervousness in a large, fortifying gulp of cognac. *You're being a jerk, Dany,* she yelled at herself.

Rambler sat down beside her on the sofa. His arms and legs were very long, but unlike some tall men, he did not slouch, nor were his movements awkward in any way. He was lithe, giving the impression of physical fitness and well-being. Dany approved. She liked tall, smooth-moving men. Even though Max Rambler sent a plethora of unsettling feelings through her, she continued to find him attractive.

"Now, Ms. Holland."

"Dany," she corrected.

"Max."

He smiled again. He was even more appealing when he smiled.

"So you're the new headmistress of St. Crispin's School," he went on. His eyes flickered over her. She was stylishly clad in a narrow gray wool skirt, two loose layers of pink and violet sweaters, patterned stockings and low-heeled gray pumps. The sweaters could hardly be thought revealing, but the skirt was somewhat short, and rode up higher than she would have liked as she sat there on his low sofa. She caught him looking at her legs. Although he was not so obvious as to be rude about it, the scrutiny added to her unease.

"I must confess that my image of you has been blasted to bits. You're a good deal younger and prettier than I expected you to be. In fact," he said, tilting his head to one side as he continued to study her, "I can hardly believe those old fogies at St. Crispin's hired you."

Dany drew herself up to sit more primly. "I'm older than I look, and I assure you I am fully qualified. I was a school administrator in the San Diego area for a number of years."

"Indeed?" The corners of his mouth lifted, as if he were amused by her defensiveness.

"Yes." Actually, she'd been a high-school English teacher for four years and an assistant principal for three, but it had *seemed* like longer.

"Edith Kenworthy, the late headmistress, had been around for centuries. I think everyone expected her replacement to be someone of similar vintage." He grinned. "I'll bet the students were delighted when they saw you."

"I hope the students have as much respect for me as they had for the venerable Mrs. Kenworthy," she said with a smile. "I wouldn't want them to think they could get away with anything just because I'm relatively young."

"Heaven forbid they should get away with anything. The place is run like a military camp."

"It certainly is not."

"You must admit that it's a far cry from your average public high school, Dany. Six hours of homework every night and no dating allowed. That's a bit extreme, don't you think?"

"Maybe so, but I know what public high schools are like nowadays. Sex, liquor, drugs, no discipline. And, unfortunately, little in the way of learning. The structured environment of St. Crispin's is far more supportive of good education, and I happen to believe that strict discipline builds character."

"Listen to you. So young, and you sound like a dictator."

Dany flushed. She realized she was coming across as a good deal more authoritarian than her personal philosophy could account for; the public high school where she'd worked for seven years hadn't been *that* bad. But Rambler made her nervous, and it was a rare feeling. She was usually more self-assured.

"Builds character, huh?" he persisted. "I'm not sure I agree with you. It may be true that barbarism has seized the public schools of America, but I think St. Crispin's errs too much the other way. Kids need a little fun now and then. I know. I had the misfortune of attending the damn school."

"You did?" Dany was surprised. She had heard various rumors about Rambler, but she had not known he was an alumnus. "When did you graduate?"

His expression darkened, and she noted that his limbs seemed to have gone tense. "Let's not get into all that," he said shortly. "You said when we spoke that you had an urgent matter to discuss with me."

"Yes." Her mind was wildly speculating. Maybe he hadn't graduated. Maybe he'd been kicked out for some reason and had borne a grudge ever since. Maybe that's why he was terrorizing her students—out of some twisted desire for revenge.

The trouble was, he'd been perfectly nice so far. Max Rambler and his spooky mansion were a little unusual, perhaps, but he didn't seem dangerous, malicious or psychotic. On the contrary, he was quite a pleasant man. Right, said a skeptical little voice inside her. So was the Boston Strangler.

"So what can I do for you, Dany? You were very insistent over the phone. What's so important that you were willing to brave an evening in my company?"

"You make it sound as if your company is something to be dreaded."

He shrugged. "I don't lead the most conventional life in the world. People react oddly to me sometimes."

"Do you really sleep during the day, or is that just part of your mystique?"

"What mystique?"

"The sinister computer whiz who knows so much about vampires that he might actually be one."

A furrow appeared in his brow. She'd obviously taken him by surprise. "Is that really what they say?" He sounded amused.

"So I'm told. You're a versatile man. Along with your high-tech wizardry you are responsible, I understand, for a game called Hunt the Night City."

Rambler groaned. "Have the kids been playing the game again? So that's the reason for this visit. They're playing, and you found out about it."

"Yes."

"Of course. I should have known." He pushed a hand through his dark hair, ruffling it. "Well? What are you going to do to them? Last time a bunch of them got caught, old lady Kenworthy suspended the lot."

"This has happened before?" She wished she'd known.

"Sure," Rambler said. He stretched his impossibly long legs out, angling them slightly in her direction, and crossed them at the ankles. He was wearing short black boots under his jeans. "Hunt the Night City appeals to adolescents, which isn't surprising, I suppose, since I was barely more than an adolescent myself when I thought it up. It was an offshoot of an earlier game called Knight of the Vampires. That's Knight with a *K*, by the way. I thought puns were the highest form of literary expression at the age of twenty-two."

Dany couldn't repress a smile. "You mean you've invented *two* board games?"

"Yeah, but Knight never caught on. Hunt the Night City, on the other hand, sold millions back in the seventies. I had a blossoming career as the next Monopoly king back then, before I decided to concentrate on microchips. Ah, the misspent days of youth."

"Are you claiming that this vampire nonsense is a thing of the past?"

He winged an eyebrow at her. "As far as I'm concerned, yes. The games I play now are far more sophisticated."

I'll bet, she thought venomously.

"What exactly is all this leading up to, Dany? If the kids at St. Crispin's are playing vampire games again, there's nothing I can do to stop them. Even if there were, it's doubtful that you'd get my cooperation. The game is melodramatic, certainly, but harmless. Why not just let them play?"

"It's not harmless."

"Of course it's harmless. Psychologically useful, too—a good way for them to get their aggressions out without hurting anybody."

"You may not continue to think so when you hear the wild claims of one of our students."

She saw the furrow in his brow again. "What do you mean? Who?"

"A boy named David Ellis. Do you know him, Mr. Rambler?"

"Max," he corrected absently. "David Ellis? No, I don't think so. Is there some reason I should?"

"He went to a lecture you were giving in town last spring. He spoke with you after it was over."

"So did a lot of kids. I can't be expected to remember every one."

"You seem to have made quite an impression on him."

"Really? Well, I was talking about robotics—the artificial intelligence project I'm working on now. I didn't tell them exactly what I'm doing, of course. That's confidential. But I discussed the theories involved. Kids love that sort of stuff."

"You've had a powerful effect on a number of our students. According to David, they're obsessed with your vampire game."

"You look and sound disapproving, Dany. But why should I feel chastened? On the contrary, I'm flattered that something I came up with so many years ago should still be stimulating kids' imaginations."

"I hardly think the stimulation is positive or desirable. David believes vampires really exist. Something about your game has convinced him."

"So? Maybe David's right."

He smiled, his teeth gleaming in the darkness.

"Come on, Max." She tried to sound nonchalant. "You're not going to sit there and tell me that you, a scientist, actually believe in the existence of vampires?"

"Why not? Even scientists have to admit that there are a lot more mysteries in this world than there are rational explanations."

She chose not to respond to this. She didn't care to have her superstitions played upon by him. The ill-lit house and those laser-beam eyes of his had done quite enough damage already. "A cult of sorts has grown up around you and your game. You remember the medieval-dungeon-game craze of a few years back? Scary things happened to some of the kids who took those fantasies too literally. I'm worried that something similar may be going on at St. Crispin's."

"Why?"

"Several of our students have been badly frightened. They're teenagers. You know what a difficult age that is. The least little thing can set them off. The master-slave scenario on which your game is based can be extremely destructive if a shy fifteen-year-old with an inferiority complex gets mixed up with a cocky seventeen-year-old with the urge to dominate."

"Particularly if one's a guy and the other's a girl," he pointed out with what she could have sworn was a certain amount of glee.

"Perhaps. Although at this point I'm not overly concerned about sexual misconduct. All the students know how strict our rules are about that."

"You and your blasted rules. At that age all they think about is sex."

Dany glared at him, but he took no notice of her disapproval as he blithely continued, "Which is probably one reason why they like the game. Vampire fantasies are blatantly sexual. The kiss on the throat. The penetration of the fangs. The heart-to-heart exchanging of the blood. To a vampire, the claiming of his victim is the ultimate erotic act. He sometimes falls deeply in love with the mortal who inspires such passion, such ecstasy."

Dany felt as if the conversation had suddenly veered out of her control. Her palms started to perspire. "A perverse and horrible ecstasy, since it ends in his victim's death."

"It need not. The vampire can sip, you know, instead of gorging. In such cases, his human partner survives to offer her throat over and over again."

His voice was so hypnotic that Dany was fascinated in spite of herself. He seemed to move a little closer to her on the couch. She caught herself staring at that sulky, sexy mouth.

"Twentieth-century vampires aren't quite so bloodthirsty as they used to be in the old days," he went on. "They don't kill as often. They can't—it's not practical. It's been a lot harder to get rid of the victim's body since the advent of modern forensic medicine. Vampires have no wish to be tracked down and eliminated, so they've learned to control their cravings for human blood. Haven't you read the booklet that comes with the board version of Hunt the Night City? It's all explained there."

She drew a shaky breath. "You're very weird, Max, you know that?"

He gave her a grin that was packed with little-boy mischief and adult male charm. "So I've been told."

She felt his physical magnetism. It seemed to radiate toward her, engaging her, disarming her. That mouth, those come-hither eyes, that crispy dark hair, something about the turn of his throat, the long, slender body with its lithe musculature . . . All the various pieces and parts of him pulled her, drew her in a manner she could never remember experiencing before with any man. Powerful. Extraordinary. Supernatural?

Oh come on, she told herself. He's attractive, that's all. And you've been celibate as a nun since the divorce went through. He stirs your poor, starving, neglected hormones . . . so what? There's nothing remarkable about that. It would be odd if you *didn't* respond.

Still, this was hardly the time to be indulging in sensual fantasy. Her hormones could darn well quiet down until she resolved the problem with David. "You say your vampire game is harmless. If so, how do you account for the fact that somebody tried to sink his teeth into David Ellis's throat the other night?"

Rambler stiffened. *"What?"*

"Yes. My student was subjected to a real version of the vampire's deadly kiss."

"They're not supposed to do that. In Hunt the Night City, the 'kill' consists of a tap on the shoulder, not a bite on the neck."

"So I understand. But David was overpowered and genuinely attacked. He said a tall man—not a kid—had come upon him in the dark and done it. He even showed me the mark."

Max muttered an obscenity. He leaned forward, his eyes intent on her face. "Is he okay?"

"Well, he's frightened, of course. He wouldn't have come to me if he hadn't been." She took a deep breath. "So you see, there's something very unpleasant going on at St. Crispin's. Teenagers are playing your game, but there must be adults involved, too. At least one, anyway. Apparently there's a character known as the Ancient One. The master vampire of them all.''

"Yes. One of the objects of the game is to become the Ancient One. But that's at a higher level; the Ancient One does not participate in every game.''

"That fits, I suppose. I suspect somebody is playing this role at St. Crispin's. He's obviously an adult, and he may be mentally unbalanced. God knows what kind of kick he gets out of this, but he's using these kids, hurting them. I intend to put a stop to it.''

"Good for you.'' His voice was very flat, and she couldn't tell whether he was impressed by her determination or mocking it. "What I still don't understand is what you want from me.''

She hesitated, trying to decide whether to add that David had named him as the attacker. It proved unnecessary. Rambler watched her closely for a few seconds, giving her the eerie feeling that he was reading her mind. Vampires were said to be able to do that, too. All the books declared that they possessed remarkable telepathic powers.

His mouth seemed to harden. "You think it's me, don't you? You came here because you suspect me of being your villain.''

She took a deep breath before confirming it. "David didn't get a very good look at his attacker's face, but yes, he tentatively identified him as you.''

"He did, did he?'' The words were clipped off. "It seems my mystique is getting a little out of hand.''

She said nothing.

"I'm amazed you came here alone tonight, Headmistress.'' His hand came out of nowhere to cup her chin. He turned her head to see her profile. His thumb brushed a stray wisp of hair off her cheek as he murmured, "If I'm unscrupulous enough to go about molesting teenagers, what's to stop me from sharpening my fangs on your lovely throat?''

Dany jerked her head away. The need to stand up and get away from him became uncontrollable. She put her cognac glass down on the antique coffee table and tried to rise, but his hand on her shoulder prevented her. He had moved very fast, sliding over to close the distance between them. The sofa sank under his weight, bringing her hip and the top of her leg against the firm muscles of his thigh. She could feel the warmth of his body. At least he *was* warm. Vampires were supposedly cold—unless they had recently drunk their nightly ration of blood.

''Don't run now, Dany. You've been very brave so far, and I was just beginning to enjoy your company.''

Her hands flew up between them. ''Stop it. You're trying to frighten me.'' And succeeding, she added wryly to herself.

He was crowding her against the arm of the sofa, his strong, graceful body much too near. ''And you just accused me of an outrageous crime against a child. How do you expect me to react to that? I've got a temper, and by God, you've just ignited it.''

''Let go of me.''

He paid no attention. One of his hands began coasting lazily through her hair. ''So what if I frighten you a little? There's a curious pleasure in it, wouldn't you agree? Why do you suppose people read scary books, play scary games? You enjoy those things yourself, don't you, Danielle?''

He couldn't possibly know her secret cravings for that kind of stimulation. Not unless he could indeed read minds. Warily, she tried to throw up walls around her psyche. But she could sense him sending out mental feelers, tendrils of thought that were almost as palpable as his fingers, his limbs.

"And why not enjoy it?" he continued in that same seductive tone. "There's an exciting rush in the heightened awareness, the pounding of the blood, the racing of the mind that you feel when you're afraid."

Dany felt the rush. It was exactly as he described. Her palms were beading, and her heart was gunning so fast she thought she might faint. His hands were on her throat now, those long-fingered, elegant hands. His face was suspended over hers, his green eyes incandescent in the dark, and that erotic mouth so close, too close.

"You're trembling, Dany."

She shut her eyes to escape that mesmerizing stare. *Vampires can fix their victims with their gaze, rendering them helpless.*

His lips lightly touched the skin at her temple. He blew a few strands of her long hair out of his way, then kissed the shell of her ear. "You're so tempting, Dany, with your red-gold hair and your sweet blue eyes and your soft, soft skin."

Why were his words so alluring, so sweet? Why did she half wish them to be true? She made a faint sound, which he ignored. He trailed a series of tantalizing kisses down from the corner of her mouth to her jawline. One hand slid down to caress a spot in the hollow of her throat. She could hear his breathing quicken. "So pretty," he whispered, lowering his head until she felt that demonic mouth hovering over the artery thundering in her neck.

"Tell me again, Dany. Are you absolutely sure you don't believe in vampires?"

Three

———

Stop it." Dany was swimming against a sucking, sensuous tide. Even though he frightened her, she felt drawn to Max Rambler. So far he hadn't actually hurt her; in fact, his strong hands were extra gentle as they rustled through her hair, loosening it from its prim chignon. Despite the threat of his languid mouth on her throat, she didn't sense any real danger.

It seemed incredible that desire could exist side by side with fear, but such was indeed the case. *What's wrong with me?* There was a subtle scent about him that appealed to her. His light, teasing kisses were stirring her senses, and those pesky hormones, denied so long, were obviously rejoicing.

His mouth was more insistent now, his kisses hot, sure and infinitely beguiling. His tongue darted out to lick her skin; then she felt something hard, the slight pressure of his teeth. Dear God, was he actually going to do it?

She let out a faint protest, appalled that it wasn't louder. Why wasn't she kicking, clawing, screaming? It wasn't like her to be so passive. What kind of power did he hold over her? *Vampires mesmerize their victims so thoroughly that they willingly offer their throat for the deadly kiss.*

"Damn you, Rambler," she said, more loudly this time. "Cut it out!"

She felt the warm exhalation of his breath. It smelled of perfume, tasted of regret. "Okay, take it easy," he said. "You're perfectly safe." Slowly, he raised his head. Her skin tingled where his teeth had touched it, but he hadn't bitten down.

"Let go of me." Dany hugged herself. She was dismayed to realize she was shaking, actually shaking. Rambler ran the back of his fingers over the burning spot on her throat, then dropped his hand and moved a few inches away. But he was still too close.

I've got to get out of here, she thought, even as she raised her gaze to his. He was smiling, a devilish, amused smile that made him look all too human. Around his eyes the laugh lines had deepened, were deepening still. "Planning to run?" he asked huskily.

Dany counted to ten, snatching at her self-control.

"Go ahead. I won't stop you."

The words were a taunt, and they broke what remained of the spell he'd cast upon her. She felt a glorious upsurge of anger. No, damn him, she wasn't going to run. He was a flesh-and-blood man, nothing more. She'd been a fool to think anything else.

"You jerk, Rambler. You think it's funny, don't you? Look at you. You scare me out of my wits, and then you laugh."

"You're lucky I'm laughing. A few moments ago I was mad enough to bite rocks, much less the tender flesh of your throat. Still, you needn't pull out the flaming pistols. I didn't hurt you, did I? I only did what you accused me of doing to David whatever-his-last-name-is. Not even that. There will be no bruise on your throat."

His words only made her angrier. It felt good. Finally, she was restored to her normal self. She'd been behaving like a lily-livered ninny ever since she'd entered this place.

"You fully expected me to scream or faint or flee from you in terror. Well, I'm not going to. I may be a little superstitious, but I'm not that easy to intimidate."

Something flashed in his face—admiration, perhaps? It was gone before she could analyze it. But he leaned forward as if she had taken on new interest for him as she added, "I came here tonight to demand an explanation from you about what's been going on at St. Crispin's, and I'm not leaving until I get one."

"That's tough, Ms. Holland, because you're not going to get an explanation from me. I don't know a damn thing about what's been going on at your posh country-club academy. And I resent being condemned without trial as some sort of power-mad high priest of vampirism who gets his kicks out of tormenting teenaged kids. What the hell right have you got to go around making accusations like that?"

"I'm not your accuser. David Ellis is."

"Since when do you listen to the hysterical claims of every single crazy kid? What is he, fifteen? Sixteen? As you yourself said, that's a difficult age. He's probably under stress, imagining things, blowing them out of proportion."

"David is a very steady boy, not the least bit hysterical."

"If he plays Hunt the Night City, he's into fantasy, he's imaginative."

"You insisted that an active imagination is perfectly normal."

"Of course it is. But I'll also admit that the game attracts players who have an active fantasy life, and that some small percentage of these people might be nut cases. You say he's normal, but look at it from my angle: he says I attacked him and I know damn well I didn't. Therefore, the kid's either crazy or a liar."

He paused for a moment before continuing, "I don't remember meeting this blasted kid, and I haven't set foot on the campus of St. Crispin's for seventeen years." He rose to his feet, grabbed her by the wrist and jerked her up to stand beside him. "Let's go."

"Ow! What are you doing?" His fingers were like a manacle, and she couldn't twist free.

"The entertainment's over for tonight."

"You mean you're throwing me out?"

"Damn right."

Dany didn't speak as Max Rambler led the way back through the darkened corridors to the front of the house. He used a flashlight this time, she noted. The candelabrum had obviously been a prop he'd used for maximum dramatic effect.

His anger seemed to be genuine. If he was guiltless in this affair, he had every right to be furious. But was he guiltless? Surely not. Any man who could take such fiendish satisfaction in frightening the wits out of a woman could not be completely free of malice.

At the front door they were joined once again by Joseph the cat, who rubbed hard against Dany's legs and meowed plaintively. Max bent down and hauled the monster into his arms. He absently rubbed the cat's ears while Dany stared at those long fingers of his, feeling awkward, still not knowing what to say. He was gentle with the cat, she noted, and the cat was affectionate toward him.

"I feel like a criminal," she admitted. "I don't think I've ever been ejected from anyone's home before."

The faintest smile turned up the corners of Max Rambler's lips. "Do you good. Builds character, as the old dragon Mrs. Kenworthy would have said."

"Look, I'm sorry if I offended you. I know I haven't been very tactful or diplomatic, but you certainly haven't come across as the soul of courtesy tonight, either."

"You're right. I'm sorry...too. Goodbye, Ms. Holland."

They were back to the formality of strangers. Too late, Dany remembered that she'd intended to ask him several specific questions about how Hunt the Night City was actually played. David's description had done no more than give her the general idea.

"These kids are important to me." She spoke softly but intensely. "That's why I came storming over here tonight. I'm responsible for them. I care about David Ellis. I care about all my students."

"Bully for you."

She sensed that he was not as callous as he sounded. "Do you have any children of your own, Mr. Rambler?"

Something tightened around his mouth, but it was too dark there in the hallway to put a name to his emotion. "No."

"Well, I do. I have a six-year-old daughter, Sarah. It's not difficult for me to project a few years into the future and imagine her as a teenager. And I'll tell you, they say women are not as violent as men, but if I ever heard that some weirdo was scaring my daughter the way the so-called Ancient One scared David, I swear I'd hunt him down and take him apart with my bare hands. Do you understand?"

Rambler said nothing for several seconds, but Dany sensed a change in him. She couldn't define it. There in the stygian blackness she could hardly even see the man. When he finally broke the silence, his words startled her: "You're not wearing a wedding ring."

"I'm no longer married."

"Divorced?"

She nodded.

"You seem young to have a child."

"I'm thirty."

"I'm several years older than you."

"So what?" She was mystified by the twist the conversation had taken.

They considered each other. Dany felt curiously reluctant to leave, and Max no longer seemed in such a hurry to throw her out. This is crazy, she thought. What a contradictory sort of man.

"Well, good night," she said. "I've got to get home to my baby-sitter. Sarah sometimes wakes up around this time. I like to be there for her. She hasn't totally adjusted, yet, to the divorce."

"May I see you again?" asked Max.

Dany blinked. "What on earth for?"

He gave her a devastating grin. Its meaning couldn't be mistaken, and the color flared up in her cheeks. Was he actually suggesting...? Yes, he was. Her hormones surged hopefully. No way, she told them. Whoa.

"I don't think so, Max. If what happened back there on your sofa is any indication of the way you make love, I can skip it, thank you very much."

"I didn't mean that. Or at least—" his charm flashed again "—that's not all I meant." He paused, seeming to chase the right words. "I'm realizing that I don't know anything about you. And that I want to."

"You're not my type," she said, all too aware that she didn't sound convincing. The chemicals inside her were clamoring, *He is, he is.*

Her refusal didn't seem to faze him. He kept right on grinning and gave her a courtly bow as he opened the door for her exit. He was still cuddling the cat, who seemed content to watch the proceedings from the crook of Rambler's arm. "Do you live in the headmistress's cottage on the St. Crispin's campus?"

"Yes, I do. Me and my six-year-old," she added, thinking another mention of the latter ought to be enough to discourage him.

It wasn't. "Don't be so sure I'm not your type, Dany. I like kids. I may drop by some evening to see you." His laugh lines deepened. "After sunset, of course."

Her own spirit lightened as she caught a glimpse of the mischief dancing in his eyes. He was no longer angry, and for that she was thankful. She was not normally antagonistic, and the conflict between them had disturbed her. "I hope you won't object to the garlic I have strung over my doorway," she said, in a playful tone that was far more representative of her usual manner with people.

"Ha. You think garlic will stop me? Sorry, Dany, but that's a myth. Utter nonsense."

"Nonsense? You mean I'm not to believe the vampire books on the subject of garlic?"

"Nope. A crucifix won't protect you either, I'm afraid. Modern vampires just laugh at such paltry attempts to keep them at bay."

"Really?" Although his own tone was light, she felt slightly disconcerted once again. She could have sworn his jade-green eyes were shining in the dark.

"Oh yes," he murmured in that low, hypnotic voice. "Nothing stops a vampire except fire or the sun."

"How about a stake through the heart?" She was determined not to let him frighten her again.

He smiled. "Now that might be true. Then again, it might not. I don't have any personal experience with stakes through the heart. Fortunately."

Bravely, she tapped her fingers on his chest. "I'll keep that in mind if we ever meet again."

"We will meet again. That I can promise you."

Terrific, she thought, not quite sure whether to be pleased or dismayed. "Good night," she said as she turned and ran down the steps to her car. When she inserted the key in the ignition and turned it, the Toyota made nothing more than a whirring sound. For a moment she thought, Oh no, please don't let me be stuck here. Then, thank goodness, the engine turned over and the headlights flashed on.

She drove in a half circle, steering toward the gravel driveway that led back down Glencrag to the school. Rambler was still standing on the top step of the gloomy mansion. For a moment her headlights trapped him in their beam. He was watching her. Even from this distance she could feel the dark energy emanating from him.

"There's no such thing as vampires," she said aloud between clenched teeth. She honked and waved nonchalantly before rounding a curve in the driveway and escaping from his sight.

When Dany got home to the small Cape-style cottage that had come with the job, she found Jennifer Stokes, the baby-sitter, who was also a student at St. Crispin's, mesmerized by the rock video that was loudly emanating from MTV. It was so loud, in fact, that Jennifer didn't hear Dany enter, and she jumped up, looking guilty, when Dany called her name.

"Oh, Ms. Holland! You're home early." The girl, who was a blooming sixteen with clear skin, pretty features, glossy dark hair and a touch too much eye makeup, rushed to turn off the television. Dany could tell she was embarrassed to be caught watching the vids. Rock music was another thing that had always been frowned upon by that ever-vigilant guardian of youthful morals, Mrs. Kenworthy. There were no stereos or TVs allowed in the dormitories of St. Crispin's.

Dany herself liked the color and energy of the videos, although she certainly wasn't about to admit this to anyone at St. Crispin's. Not yet, anyway. The truth was, Dany hoped to change some of the more stringent policies of her predecessor, but instinct warned her to move slowly. It was too soon to start shaking things up.

"It's okay, Jennifer, I don't mind your watching a little TV. Just don't turn it up so loud in future. I want you to be able to hear Sarah if she cries. How was she tonight? Did she wake up?"

"No, Ms. Holland. She was perfect. I checked her lots of times, but she didn't make a sound."

"Let me just run up and take a look before I see you home."

Sarah was sleeping on her side with her favorite fingers in her mouth and a stuffed puppy clutched to her chest. Dany brushed a lock of wispy gold hair off her daughter's cheek and kissed her forehead. Sarah didn't stir. She had turned six in the spring and was attending first grade this year in Chesterton. Every morning Dany would take her out to the bus, which Sarah was extremely proud to be riding. She carried a pink lunch box and wore a navy-blue backpack that contained her dry shoes and her pencil case. She thought herself extremely grown-up.

"Good night, my love," Dany whispered, adjusting the blankets over her daughter's slender body. She kissed her once again, then went downstairs to Jennifer.

Carefully locking the house behind her, Dany walked Jennifer to the corner. Fortunately, her dorm was only a few hundred yards away. Jennifer always said she needn't bother, but Dany insisted. Particularly now, with a would-be vampire running around.

She could not resist asking Jennifer if she knew anybody at school who played Hunt the Night City.

The girl seemed startled. "You mean the vampire game? A lot of people play it. It's pretty popular, the board game, I mean."

"I was referring to the version where everybody takes a part and acts out the fantasies. I understand some of the kids play the game, in that manner, on the campus at night."

Jennifer refused to meet Dany's eyes. "I don't know about that, Ms. Holland. How could they? I mean, there's an eleven o'clock curfew."

Dany wasn't sure what the curfew had to do with it. "It gets dark long before eleven o'clock, so I don't imagine that would stop them."

"Well, yes, but—"

"But what?"

"Playing the game's against the rules. Nobody I know wants to get in trouble."

She knew something; Dany could tell. Evidently she was reluctant to talk about it. It was one of the things Dany liked least about her job. Mrs. Kenworthy had these kids so intimidated that it was almost impossible to get them to talk. David had been the exception. "You're a friend of David Ellis, aren't you?" It had been David, in fact, who'd recommended Jennifer for the baby-sitting job.

"Yes." Jennifer was twisting a dark lock of hair around her fingers and trying to sound nonchalant. "Why?"

"Would you say that he's an overly imaginative boy who tends to get caught up in his fantasies?"

"David? No, not really. I mean, he's a good actor in the drama club and all, but he's also very down-to-earth."

"Is David having any particular problems that you know of? With his schoolwork, with his friends, with girls?"

Once again, Jennifer looked shifty-eyed. "God, I've no idea, Ms. Holland."

Dany knew kids well enough to realize she wouldn't get any more out of the girl tonight. Anyway, she'd left Sarah alone too long.

She cast a glance back at the cottage. Her mind always seemed to seize upon the most ridiculous thoughts during the few minutes when she had to leave Sarah alone in the house. A prowler would slip inside, steal her child and vanish into the night. The house would spontaneously burst into flame and Sarah would be trapped. Or, a little less melodramatic but agonizing nonetheless, the little girl would wake up, frightened from a nightmare, run downstairs to find Mommy and discover she'd been left alone. The possibilities for disaster seemed endless, particularly to a mother of Dany's imaginative cast of mind. It was at these moments that she genuinely hated Greg for abandoning them.

"I'd better get back now, Jennifer. Good night."

"Ms. Holland? David's not in any trouble, is he?"

Dany assured her he was not. She waited until Jennifer got safely inside her dorm, then hurried home. Although she was usually cavalier about locks, tonight Dany made sure all the doors and windows were tightly bolted before she retired to bed.

Long after Dany's car had pulled away, Max Rambler lingered outside on the front steps of his house, gazing into the night. It seemed he could still see the way the new headmistress's luxuriant coppery hair had caught the light from the car's interior and flamed around her face. He remembered the silken texture of that hair, which had come loose from its prim knot when he'd caressed her, clinging to his palms and winding itself around his fingers like an animate creature. Soft hair, delicate but fiery, like the woman it adorned.

He conjured up the scent of her, the taste of her. Her low-pitched, sexy voice. Her tentative, trembling response to him despite that nasty trick he'd pulled on her—the confirmation that she'd felt the attraction as intensely as he had. Oh yes. Ms. Danielle Holland had come across about as passionate as a drainpipe at the start of their interview, but by the end of it he'd begun to have a glimmering of the true dimensions of her sensuality and spirit.

Too bad he'd blown it by losing his temper. Clearly, that had not been one of his smoother moves.

"So what d'you think, Joe, old boy?" he muttered to the fat ball of fur who was still lolling in his arms. He scratched him hard behind the ears. The purring increased. "She's pretty, isn't she? I like the way she moves, all graceful and flowing, her hips so slender and her legs so long. Nice breasts, too, but you wouldn't appreciate that, Joseph, would you? She likes cats, though, you can be grateful for that. The last couple of females I set my snares for had no use for you, if you'll recall."

The big cat kneaded his master's forearm with his sharp claws and opened his mouth in a silent, dainty yawn.

"You don't think we scared her too much, do you? I've really got to watch that. It's my damn temper, Joe." He laughed shortly. "You'd think by this time I'd know better."

The cat turned his head and gave his master an arch glance.

"Don't say it," said Max. "I'm no good for her, right? I shouldn't be thinking the things I'm thinking. I should back off, repress my baser instincts, exercise a little self-control." He shrugged and smiled. "That's the philosophy they teach at St. Crispin's, old pal. It never did work too well on me."

The thought of St. Crispin's and everything that had passed there all those years ago sobered him considerably. "Damn her," he said in an infinitely more threatening tone. "She doesn't have any idea what she's tangling with. And she won't find out, either, not if I can help it. I won't have the past dredged up again.''

The big cat purred, not the least bit interested.

''You wouldn't hesitate if a fat, juicy bird fell into your path, would you, Joe? You'd simply tear its throat and feast.''

As if reminded of its stomach, the big cat squirmed and jumped down. It stared for a moment into the woodland, then glided down the stairway to begin its nocturnal prowling. Max Rambler remained in the doorway for several minutes longer, listening to the soft breathings and scurryings of the forest. He tilted back his head, gazing up at the thousands of bright stars that danced across the firmament. The velvet darkness settled around him, a familiar feeling, comforting somehow. He thrust his hands into his pockets, pulled the front door shut behind him, and followed his cat into the inky depths of night.

Four

After getting Sarah safely off to school the next morning, Dany walked down the lane to Adams Hall, the administration building where the headmistress's office was located. The morning was clear and bright, the sky a vivid blue and the trees burning with the red, golds and orange flames of autumn. On such a day it seemed ridiculous to fret about dark deeds that were done by night.

The campus was beautiful. Dany had fallen in love with the place from the moment she'd first arrived for her interview and seen St. Crispin's nestled in an emerald valley in the foothills of the White Mountains, its gray stone buildings shimmering in the sunlight like some peaceful thirteenth-century manor. The school had been constructed seventy-five years before by an architect influenced by such Gothic structures as the cathedral of Notre Dame. The effect was lushly medieval. The buildings were cool and dark, with high ceilings and graceful arches. The chapel even had flying buttresses.

Dany climbed the wide stone steps leading into Adams Hall, her briefcase under her arm. She was just about to enter her office on the first floor when she nearly collided with her administrative assistant, Casper Pearson, who was on his way out. "Oh, here you are," he said. "I've been looking for you."

"I'm not late, am I?"

"No, I guess not. But I was worried." Cass was dressed in jeans and a black leather jacket that had seen better days. His brown hair was tipped with blond and punked. He had a small gold stud in one ear. Dany knew his appointment had raised some eyebrows around campus. Mrs. Kenworthy's assistants had always been prim, proper and female.

"Worried? Why?"

"I wanted to make sure you were still in one piece after your visit to the vampire."

"As you see," she said, laughing, "I seem to have survived."

"Unless he's turned you into a vampire too."

"I wouldn't be out and about by daylight if he had."

"True. I forgot about that. But tell me, did he try to pounce upon your throat?"

Dany was certainly not about to confirm that Max Rambler had done exactly that. The story would appeal all too vividly to her assistant's innate sense of drama.

Cass was twenty-three, a college dropout who could type ninety words per minute and use every word-processing system known to man. He was a whiz at all the details of office management that Dany hated to attend to herself—he could organize anything from a file cabinet to a formal dinner for five hundred alumni. He was also very good at research, particularly if the subject was the least bit unusual or bizarre. Investigating Max Rambler had been a joy for him.

"Mr. Rambler is not our culprit, Cass. He denies knowing David, and he was pretty angry by the time I'd made it clear what I was accusing him of."

"He would deny it, I suppose, if he were guilty. You didn't expect him to come right out and admit it, did you?"

"No, but I believe him. I think."

"You think?"

Dany sat down behind her desk and rested her chin in her hands. Her dreams during the night had been troubled. Was her subconscious mind trying to warn her to be careful? Not to be so trusting? Was danger gathering around her, or were her long-denied desires simply acting up, causing this restlessness deep inside her?

"Did you know Rambler was a student at St. Crispin's seventeen years ago?"

Cass's eyes dilated. "You're kidding."

"No. Do we have a file on him, do you suppose?"

"If he was a student, we have a file."

"Where would it be?"

"In the archives, probably. Down in the basement with the other inactive stuff."

"I'd like to have a look at it if you can find it for me, Cass. And pull David Ellis's records for me, too, okay?"

"My pleasure," said Cass. "I'll get on it right away."

Dany summoned David to her office during a break between his classes. This time she had his records in front of her, but they didn't help her much. He had transferred last spring to St. Crispin's from a private school in Seattle when his mother, an interior designer named Olivia Ellis, had moved her business to Boston. There was no mention of his father on David's school records. Mrs. Ellis had listed her marital status as divorced.

David's grades at his former boarding school had been just as good as his grades at St. Crispin's. He'd been on the fencing team. Here he had joined the drama club.

"I saw Mr. Rambler last night," she told him without preamble. "He's a little strange, but I doubt he's your vampire, David. Certainly he denied it strenuously enough."

"You mean you actually accused him of attacking me?"

"Well, yes. I went to his house last night and laid the whole story before him."

"You went to his house? By yourself?" He looked horrified. "But Ms. Holland, I told you—"

"David, listen to me." Dany had decided to take a tougher stance with the boy. If he'd by any chance been making the whole thing up, maybe he'd think twice about pursuing it. "Mr. Rambler was very angry when he heard that you and your friends have built this outlandish mystique around him. I can't say that I blame him. Do you know what slander is, David? By accusing someone without proof, you are defaming their character."

David was silent. He seemed a little flushed.

"I need some information from you."

"What d'you mean?" He was shuffling now, looking as if he'd like nothing better than to escape.

"I mean names, David. I want to know who else plays Hunt the Night City with you on this campus. I want a complete list, not only of the people involved but also of the times you play, the places you play, the—"

"I can't," David interrupted. He looked miserable. "I didn't think you'd ask for anything like that. I mean, you didn't the other day, so I thought it was okay, you wouldn't press me. Surely you see I can't betray my friends. That would be really low."

"I'm trying to help you, David. I can't do that without additional information."

"But Ms. Holland—"

"From what you've told me, it seems some of these friends of yours might be in some danger. I'm certainly not going to permit some psycho to go around terrorizing my students. It was your decision to come to me in the first place about this matter."

"I just don't want to get anybody in trouble. I don't want anybody to get expelled because of me."

"I'm not planning to expel anybody, I assure you. I just want this nonsense stopped. This game is played in the dark, right? At night?"

"Mostly on the weekends. We study during the week, you know. I mean, we *do* study."

"Well, that's a relief," she said dryly. "But I still can't believe the security guards wouldn't have had something to report before this if a bunch of kids were playing Hunt the Night City on the campus grounds every weekend."

"We play in a place where the guards never see us. Anyway, after midnight, security's pretty lax."

"After midnight?" Jennifer's words flashed back to her. "But St. Crispin's has an eleven o'clock curfew, after which all the dorms and other campus buildings are locked."

David said nothing. He bit his lip and avoided her gaze.

"Talk, David!"

"I can't," he whispered. "I've said too much already. Oh, jeez, I knew I shouldn't have come to you."

Dany remembered the code of honor among David's age-group—you didn't rat on your friends. There weren't many crimes that were worse than that. "All right, I won't twist your arm. But I warn you, what I don't know I intend to find out."

"It's the Ancient One you should go after, not the kids," David said sullenly. "And I still say it's Max Rambler."

He was extraordinarily stubborn on that point, Dany noted. "You can go now. I have to be alone so I can think."

The boy hesitated at the door to her office. "Ms. Holland?"

"Yes?"

"You're not going to go after him by yourself, are you? Going alone to Rambler's house and all—I never thought you'd do something like that. I mean, you're young, and—and pretty...." He stopped, blushing. "The kids like you. We wouldn't want anything to happen to you."

"Thanks for your concern." She could hear the exasperation in her own voice. "You needn't worry. I've no intention of going after the Ancient One by myself. I might just ask Max Rambler to join the hunt himself, since he's the person who started all this vampire nonsense."

Dany wasn't sure what made her say this, but David reacted sharply: "That's crazy! What if he has you fooled? Vampires are clever, you know, and they can be very disarming. Why won't you listen to me, Ms. Holland? What if he *is* the Ancient One? I've heard some strange things about that man, believe me."

Dany pointed to the door. "Out, David, before I sit you in the corner with a dunce cap on your head."

But when he was gone, she put her head down on her arms and thought about vast, unlighted houses, strong fingers, wickedly tempting lips and luminescent green eyes that had seemed particularly enamored of the pulse point on her throat.

After a busy day spent interviewing candidates to replace a history professor who was retiring, Dany left her office, walked home to get her car and drove to the nearest shopping center. She found a store that sold copies of the board version of Hunt the Night City. While she was at it, she bought Sarah the new Barbie doll that her daughter had been asking for ever since she'd seen it advertised on TV. When she picked up her daughter at the day-care center where she stayed every day after school, the six-year-old immediately spotted the bag in the back seat. "Is that a toy for me, Mommy?"

"Yes. I got you a new Barbie."

"Oh neat!" She wrestled the doll out of its wrapper and clutched it to her chest. "Can we play Barbies tonight? You can use my old one." She fingered the slinky evening gown her new doll was wearing. "We can pretend they're going to Cinderella's ball."

"Okay, sweetheart. We'll play after supper."

Sarah peered at Hunt the Night City with its black cover and Gothic lettering. "What's that? It looks spooky."

"That's a toy for me."

Sarah thought this was a riot. "Oh, Mom. You're too old to play with toys."

Sarah was even more pleased when supper turned out to be her favorite—fast-food kiddie meal. Dany felt the bad-mother guilts that had been plaguing her off and on since she and Sarah had been on their own. She tried to provide her daughter with a decent home-cooked meal every day, but there were times when it was impossible. It wasn't easy, trying to be Supermom.

"Now can we play?" Sarah asked as she fed her plastic cartons and bags into the trash can.

"Get undressed and brush your teeth first, sweetheart."

"Aw, Mom—"

"Quick. Then we'll play for a while before bed instead of reading stories."

While her daughter was upstairs getting ready for bed, Dany slit the cellophane and opened Hunt the Night City. Inside she found a lurid board painted in various shades of purple, crimson and black. She spread it all out on the dining room table. On the left side was a stately stone mansion whose cellars were lined with ornately carved sarcophagi. This, apparently, was the lair of the master vampires. On the right was a less prestigious-looking resting ground—subterranean catacombs complete with piles of bones and grinning skulls. At the top of the board was a sultry turn-of-the-century city—New Orleans, perhaps. The area was marked by cafés and wharves, warehouses and seedy bars, and a tall, sinister figure leaning against a gas lamppost eyeing the throat of a passing streetwalker.

The bottom portrayed a torture chamber, complete with iron staples set in stone, a nasty-looking rack and a thug with a cat-o'-nine-tails in his fist. The center of the board to which several serpentine paths were leading, was dominated by a golden tower lined with precious metals, jewels and other symbols of earthly power.

Good heavens, Dany thought. What kind of dark imagination had created this? She had an image of Max Rambler, his handsome, autocratic features, his wicked eyes, his sensual mouth. The creature leaning against the lamppost reminded her unpleasantly of him.

"I'm ready, Mommy."

Dany quickly closed the board. Hunt the Night City was too lurid for Sarah, particularly at this time of day, just before bed. Her daughter had been having an occasional troubled night, still grieving over the divorce. Greg hadn't been a caring or sensitive father. He'd been too busy clawing his way up in the business world to have much time to spend with his family, but Sarah missed him terribly nevertheless. "Got your dolls? Okay, let's play."

Sarah handed her the old one, the one with the midnight-black hair, while she assumed control of the new, blond one. "They're going to Cinderella's ball. Here, in the castle."

She commandeered the coffee table to play the role of the castle. "It's a beautiful castle, a big gray stone building that looks a little spooky at night. See? And it's surrounded by pure green fields and huge mountains."

Dany realized her daughter was describing St. Crispin's.

"They go into the castle—come on, Mom, make your doll come in—and sing and dance and play all night."

"Sarah, where's your Ken doll? They need somebody to dance with. He can take turns dancing with them."

The little girl looked pained. "I don't like that stupid doll."

"Why not? It'll be fun. He can be the prince."

Sarah's eyes widened and her lips seemed to tremble. "There isn't any prince in this castle, Mommy."

"Sweetheart, what's the matter? Why isn't there a prince?" Dany asked, although she could guess what the answer would be. A sharp pain twisted inside her as she remembered the day Greg had left. When Sarah had understood what was happening, she'd run after her father and tackled him around the legs. "Don't go, Daddy, don't go!" she'd whispered. Her father had pried her small arms from around his knees, climbed into his car and driven off, leaving the child huddled in the driveway, weeping.

"There was one," Sarah said bitterly, "but he went away. Anyhow, it's a stupid idea. Everyone knows there's no such thing as princes, not real ones anyway."

"Oh, baby," Dany began, reaching out to pull her daughter into her arms. Sarah pressed her face to her mother's chest, still clutching her new doll. "There are princes, my darling. It's just that princesses like us sometimes have a hard time finding the right one."

"I want my daddy," Sarah whispered. "I want my daddy to come home."

"I know you want him, lovey. Of course you want him. But your mommy and daddy are divorced, and he's not going to come home. Still, you'll see him sometimes, sweety. You'll see him at Christmas, as a matter of fact, so don't cry." She paused a moment, then added, even though she wasn't sure it was true, "Your daddy loves you very much, Sarah."

"He doesn't love me. He loves his stupid new wife, that's who he loves. I hate her! I wish she'd die!"

"Oh sweetheart, it's okay to be angry, but it's not okay to wish somebody would die." For an instant Dany remembered how bloodthirsty she'd felt when she'd first found out that, busy though he was, Greg had somehow managed to squeeze in an extramarital affair. "Your mother and father couldn't live together anymore, as I've explained to you before. That happens sometimes. It's very sad, but sometimes sad things happen in life."

"I hate her," the child repeated. "And I hate him for leaving us and marrying her."

"Now that your parents are divorced, it's normal for your father to want to marry again," Dany said, trying to sound as charitable as possible. "Men and women fall in love and get married all the time. You mustn't hate your new stepmother; she's really very nice."

"Are you going to fall in love and get married again, Mom?" Sarah demanded.

"I don't know, lovey. Maybe, someday. We'll see."

"I hope you do. I want a stepfather as well as a stepmother. I want you to find a prince for us, Mommy."

The words were no sooner out of the little girl's mouth than Dany felt a prickle on the back of her neck. Eyes, she felt eyes. That odd sensation of someone watching. Superstition again, she told herself firmly even as she snapped her head around.

Across the living room from where they were sitting was a pair of ornate French doors that opened into the garden. Dany had never liked the French doors; even with the latch on they were too easy to open. Was the latch on now?

Chesterton was a small town without much crime, and unless she was in the middle of a terrifying horror novel,

Dany didn't worry excessively about intruders. But the icy fear she felt now was very similar to the sort of thing she experienced toward the climax of an exciting plot. Only more intense, because this was *real*.

Somebody was out there, she was sure of it. As she watched, one hand at her throat, the other clutching her daughter, she saw something move. There was a shadow by the French doors, a tall, slender silhouette just on the other side of the ornate glass. "Sarah. Go upstairs to your bedroom, please, and close the door."

Alerted by her mother's tone, the girl raised her head. "Why? What's the matter, Mommy?"

"Just do it, Sarah."

But the French doors were already opening, and she thought, dammit, there's no time. Dany jumped up, dragging Sarah with her, with the intention of fleeing out the front door and screaming for the neighbors. Certainly she was not going to allow herself and her daughter to be trapped in the house with the menacing shadow who was even now invading her living room. She could see a pale face and pale hands, but otherwise the apparition was entirely clothed in black. That end of the room was too ill-lit for her to be able to make out his features.

"Get out of here!" she cried, shielding her daughter with her body.

"Don't panic, Dany," said a husky, amused voice. "It's only me."

"Rambler," she breathed.

"Who else?" he said cheerfully as he glided across the room toward her.

Five

————

Mommy! Who's that?"

"Shh, Sarah, it's all right. Are you crazy?" she half shouted at Max. "You scared me! You scared my daughter."

"I'm sorry. I didn't know your daughter would still be awake. Hi, Sarah," he said, smiling at the little girl. "My name's Max."

Still clinging to her mother, Sarah looked him up and down. Max was wearing charcoal pants and a gray sweater under a black nylon windbreaker. His hair was agreeably windblown, and his eyes were greener than ever.

"Why couldn't you have come to the front door, like a normal person?" Dany snapped, angry at the fright he had given her. Her heart was still somersaulting in her chest. She must have been more affected by David Ellis's wild tales than she'd realized.

"I was coming to the front door. But as I passed the house I caught a glimpse of your hair shimmering behind the glass of the French doors, and it struck me that this way was more direct."

He glanced back at the doors and frowned. "You ought to have drapes in here, you know. Or at least a lock on those doors." With casual aplomb, he leaned down to kiss Dany's cheek, quite as if they were the oldest of friends. "You're looking very lovely tonight, Dany."

"Are you a friend of my mother's?" Sarah asked. The kiss had apparently convinced her that Max was no stranger. She disengaged her arms from around Dany's neck and moved a little away from her. She was not a particularly shy child, Dany reminded herself. On the contrary, Sarah was open to new people, new experiences. But Dany wasn't entirely sure she wanted her daughter to be open to Max.

"Yes," he said. "Soon to be a friend of yours too, I hope. What a pretty doll you have there. Is she a Barbie?"

"Yes. She's brand new. My mother got her for me today."

"May I hold her?"

"Okay."

Dany could tell at once that Max had a way with kids. He took the doll that Sarah handed him and admired her. He proved to be remarkably well versed on the subject of children's toys. "I'll bet you don't know what this is," Sarah said, pulling a bizarre object out of her toy box in the corner.

"Sure I do. May I try it?" He took the robot-shaped object and manipulated it until it turned into a wicked-looking ray gun. "I love these things," he said, brandishing it.

When they'd finished discussing her toys, Max asked Sarah about school, listening attentively to her answers. He didn't stoop or condescend; neither was he too hearty in his attentions. He simply expressed his interest, speaking directly to Sarah as if he respected her individuality, her distinctness from her mother. She responded tentatively at first, then with greater warmth. By the time Dany succeeded in prying her away and getting her upstairs to bed, Sarah was full of his praises. "I like Max, Mom," she said as she undressed for the night. "Is he a prince, do you think?"

"No, sweetheart, Max is not a prince."

When Dany returned to the first floor after getting Sarah settled down, she found that Rambler had abandoned the living room for the small library in the back of the house. It was a wonderful room, wall-to-wall books. Dany often curled up there in the leather-covered easy chair with one of her favorite horror novels. "My daughter thinks you're a prince."

"What a family. She thinks I'm a prince, you think I'm a vampire. Sounds like the two of you have been reading too many bedtime stories. Speaking of which, I've discovered your secret vice."

Dany caught a glimpse of the volume in Rambler's hands. It was Anne Rice's *Interview With The Vampire*. "I've no idea what you're talking about," she said archly.

"Oh, no? You've got three entire shelves of Gothic fantasy here, everything from *The Castle Of Otranto* to the complete works of Stephen King."

"The house was provided for me, you know. Most of the books were already here when I arrived."

"Not these books," he said gleefully. "They're all inscribed with your name. Well thumbed, too. No wonder you know all the myths about vampires—you're a fan! What would all your well-disciplined, straitlaced students think? You're really into this stuff, aren't you?"

It seemed silly to continue to feign innocence when he had the evidence right there in his hands. Instead she said, "I leave you alone for ten minutes and you tap the secrets of my soul." She advanced upon him, arms akimbo. "If you tell anybody I'll suck *your* neck. The trustees would not approve, I'm certain of that."

"What business is it of theirs what you read?"

"I'd just as soon not cross them at present. For some reason they think I'm the next Edith Kenworthy. I'm not, of course, but I like my job and I want to keep it."

"Yes, of course, your job." There was a harsh edge to his voice. "There are many ways to control people, and Edith Kenworthy knew them all. But I shouldn't have thought her baleful influence would extend over what her successor reads on her own time."

"It doesn't, obviously." She was puzzled by the intensity of his feelings on the subject. "I read what I like to read. I just don't care to shout my preferences from the rooftops, that's all."

"I hate people who won't stand up and defend their rights. I didn't think you were such a wimp."

Dany took a steadying breath. "I'm not sure what you're talking about, Max, but somehow I doubt it has anything to do with me."

That stopped him. The slightest evidence of a flush seemed to creep over Rambler's skin, flood his face briefly, then recede. "You're right. I'm sorry. How I feel about Edith Kenworthy and her hypocritical philosophy has nothing to do with you."

Why hypocritical? Dany wondered. Hadn't the good woman practiced what she preached?

Rambler pushed a hand through his dark hair, leaving it agreeably ruffled. "Anyway, the old gorgon's dead now. I, for one, don't miss her."

Clearly. He had hated Edith Kenworthy, it seemed.

Dany sat on the love seat in the corner, but when Max promptly joined her she wished she'd had the sense to choose another spot. He was altogether too close. "Do you mind my asking what my predecessor did to you?"

There was a gleam of emotion in his eyes that his dark lashes quickly curtained. "I'd rather not get into that."

Okay, mystery man, she thought, baffle me. "You were very good with Sarah," she said after a short pause. "How do you know so much about toys?"

"I still own stock in the company that marketed Hunt the Night City. They make toys as well as games. I read their quarterly reports; I like to keep up with the business trends, to make sure they're not losing my money."

This reminded her of something else Casper Pearson had told her about Max Rambler. He was apparently quite wealthy. "Made a fortune when he was just out of grad school by starting a small computer company that was instrumental in the development of microprocessors," Cass had reported. "He's one of the silicon-chip barons. The business world was shocked a couple of years ago when he quit his job as president of MicroDyne and retired to the country."

"Why did he quit?" she'd asked.

"As I heard it, he didn't care for administrative work. Said he was an inventor, not a businessman. Said he couldn't endure the high pressure and the stress any longer. People say he's still inventing in his basement, that he's about to revolutionize the field of robotics. But I don't know. Other people say he cracked under the strain and has never been the same since. Did he seem cracked to you?"

"No," Dany had answered. "Unconventional yes, but not crazy."

As for Max's school records, Cass hadn't located them yet. "They're probably in some carton with the other dead files. It may take me a while, but I'll dig 'em out."

One fact they had established: Max had not actually graduated from St. Crispin's. If he'd really been a student there, he must have either withdrawn or been expelled.

"What are you thinking?" asked Max.

Dany was jolted out of her musings. "I was, uh, wondering what you were doing here tonight."

"I told you I'd come." His voice had assumed a husky quality, and those hypnotic eyes of his moved luxuriously over her. Taken together they conveyed a meaning that was impossible to mistake. Dany felt a curl of heat in the pit of her belly. Those darn hormones again!

"And I told you I'm not interested," she said as convincingly as she could.

He stretched an arm out behind her on the back of the love seat. He wasn't touching her, but she felt hemmed in. "I guess I'm hoping you'll change your mind."

"You're pretty confident of your attractions, aren't you?"

That furrow she'd noticed the night before appeared briefly in his brow. "Not at all. I wish I were more confident, as a matter of fact. It's been a while since I've—" He stopped, looking flustered, which had the effect of endearing him far more to Dany than a smoother line would have done. "I don't run around with a lot of different women," he finished. "I'm something of a recluse, as you saw for yourself."

"And shy, no doubt?" she said archly, teasing him.

"A bit, yes."

He sounded serious, which surprised her. Until now she certainly wouldn't have characterized him as the diffident type.

He changed the subject slightly. "Your daughter misses her father, doesn't she? I heard what she said about wishing Mommy would find her a stepfather."

"Are you by any chance volunteering for the job?"

"Nope." He sent a dazzling smile her way. "But I wouldn't mind being Mommy's very close friend for a while." He allowed his fingers to graze her shoulder, sending trills of sensation all the way down to her toes. Shy? Sure.

"Unlike some men, I'm not put off by a woman with family responsibilities. I've always wanted kids of my own, as a matter of fact."

"Then why aren't you married?"

He shrugged. "Never found the right woman, I guess." He left a pause. "Your daughter's a darling. We could do some things together, the three of us." His voice dropped into a lower register. "And some other things, just you and I."

He was bone-tinglingly sexy, and Dany had to be very firm with herself. She forced her mind to focus on Sarah, who was still suffering the effects of her father's desertion. "I see. Uncle Max. The second in a series of temporary daddies, I suppose?"

"Now just a minute, Dany—"

"No, thanks. I think I'd be better off sticking to men who are put off by children for a while. Sarah's had a hard time of it, losing her father. I'd hate to give her a charmer like you for a few weeks, then watch her world collapse again when you move on."

Max looked abashed. Dany gave him a few seconds to respond, but he did not. Why am I being so sharp-tongued with him? she asked herself. Why was she trying to drive him away? He was right; men who liked children were few and far between. At this rate she wouldn't be surprised to see him get up and walk out. Was that what she wanted? Oh God, she didn't *know* what she wanted.

To her relief, Max did nothing of the sort. Instead he changed the subject again. "I had another reason for coming to see you, Dany. I thought about it after you left last night and decided I might be of help to you in tracking down the mischief-maker on your campus. The Ancient One, if that's who he's imitating. After all, I know the game better than anyone else.''

Now it was her turn to feel abashed. He kept proving himself to be a far more pleasant man than she had originally estimated. ''Thank you, but there's no reason why you should be dragged into this. Especially after the way I treated you last night.''

He shrugged off her implicit apology. ''Some weirdo has taken my vampire fantasy and turned it into a threat, something it was never meant to be. I feel an obligation to put a stop to that. Did you talk to the kid with the bruised throat again?''

''Yes, but he wasn't particularly forthcoming. Seems he doesn't want to get his friends in trouble.'' She related the details of her conversation with David. ''He implied there was some secret place where they play this game of yours. I suppose that's possible—it's a big campus and there are several empty buildings. But if it's true they play after curfew, that baffles me. The buildings are locked at eleven, and I can't believe these kids are running around with master keys.''

Max nodded, as if this was exactly what he had expected to hear.

''Do you know where they play?'' she asked.

''I can make a pretty good guess. Things haven't changed much, I suspect, since I was a student here.''

''What do you mean?''

''I'd rather show you than tell you.'' He glanced toward the stairs that led to the second floor. ''It would mean going out on the campus. Could you get a baby-sitter for Sarah?''

''Not tonight; it's too late. I've got one coming tomorrow night, though. I have to go to a faculty meeting, but I'll be free when it's over. Around eight-thirty—is that okay?''

"Sure. Tomorrow night it is. In the meantime—" He turned his body toward her with a decidedly lecherous gleam in his eyes.

But Dany was quick to sabotage his plans. "In the meantime, I have a task for you. You can give me a lesson on how to play Hunt the Night City."

She jumped up from the love seat and led the way to the dining room, where the various pieces of the game were still spread out on the table. "I bought your game today, but I haven't read the directions yet."

Max sighed. "Vampires it is."

Two hours later they were still hunched over the board, and Dany had to admit she was hooked. She rolled the dice—they were black with red spots—and came up with two threes. "Ha!" she cried and moved her piece—a slender female creature with hair like snakes—onto a gold sarcophagus square. "Doubles, Rambler. You become my slave."

"Not again," he groaned. "Why do I get the feeling you're deriving an inordinate amount of satisfaction from this game? You've already sucked the life out of one of my creatures and turned two others into vampire slaves."

"Can I help it if you're unlucky?"

"I'm going to get you for this."

Dany had picked up the rudiments of the game easily. Each player began with six creatures, three human and three undead. Those who were human tried to circle the board and make it safely back to their refuge in the city. If they met a vampire along the way, they could either flee or attack. Depending on what number they threw, and what charms or weapons they possessed, they might either survive or be drained of all their blood.

The undead creatures went the opposite way around the board, seeking refuge in the golden sarcophagi, the one place where a vampire was always safe, both from human vampire hunters and from his own kind. Vampires were more powerful than humans, although they were not entirely safe from them, particularly if caught in an unsecured grave when the sun rose. But they had little power against the master vampires, who were impervious to any kind of attack and always desirous of new servants.

An undead creature could become a master vampire if he successfully negotiated the obstacles that led to the golden tower in the center of the board. Once there, he could become all-powerful by entering the tower and challenging the Ancient One. If he failed to defeat the Ancient One in the Duel of Dominance, he was condemned to the chamber of horrors—the dungeon.

"You mean vampires can feel pain?" Dany had asked when she heard this.

"Sure. Infernal pain, lasting forever since they very seldom die."

Human creatures could be sent to the dungeon, too. "They don't last so long," Max said cheerfully. "Either they die under torture or some vampire comes along and relieves them of their blood."

"How did you ever think this stuff up?"

"Ah, shucks, I'm just kinky, I guess."

So far, Dany was doing better than Max. She had only lost one of her creatures—an unfortunate human who'd been pounced upon by one of Max's undeads—and two of her undeads had already become masters. If she could just get her other two humans back to the city and her other undead safely into the sarcophagi, she'd win this round.

Her luck abruptly ran out when Max outthrew her five times in a row. One of his slave vampires managed to defeat one of her humans, even though his powers had been sapped by slavery. Then he got his remaining undead into the tower where it was transformed into a master. He brought this creature out again, to hunt her.

Dany had to unearth her snake-haired female, who Max quickly challenged to a Dominance Duel. Dany threw a two to Max's five, then a six to Max's ten. Her female master was defeated.

"Ha! To the dungeon with her," said Max, gloating.

"No!" Dany cried. The urgency in her own voice startled her. She was really getting into this silly game.

So was her opponent. "Absolutely. That she-witch has caused me enough trouble to last a millenium or two."

"You could be merciful and let her go."

"Fat chance," he said. "Bring on the whips and chains."

"Mommy?" said a small voice from the doorway behind them. Dany abandoned her attempt to keep her snake-haired piece from falling into Max's evil clutches. Sarah was standing on the stairs, clutching her stuffed puppy. Her feet were bare, and her hair was falling into her eyes. "I had a bad dream," she whispered, her bottom lip trembling.

Dany jumped up from the table and rushed to take the child in her arms. "It's okay, sweetheart. You're safe; I'm here."

Max followed her to the stairs. When he was sure Sarah wasn't afraid of him, he reached out and gently patted her head. "Hi, Sarah," he said in the most sympathetic voice Dany had ever heard issue from his lips. "You okay?"

The golden head nodded, face still pressed to Mommy's shoulder. "There were monsters in my dream."

"Ah. Did you run away from them?"

"One I ran from. The other I kicked in the stomach."

"Clever girl," said Max. "I'll bet when you grow up you'll fight monsters just as bravely as your mommy."

"Yes," said the child, yawning hugely. "My mommy's very brave."

"Come on, love. I'll take you back upstairs and tuck you in." Dany spoke a little stiffly. Max's manner toward Sarah disconcerted her. He seemed sincere, but after all, she barely knew him. What if being nice to the child was nothing more than a ploy to aid in his seduction of the mother? She'd made it clear to him that she didn't want Sarah hurt.

"Good night, Sarah," he said as Dany carried her daughter up the stairs to her room. "Sleep tight."

"Night, Max."

Max stared after them, long after the staircase and upper hallway were empty. He'd sensed Dany's reservations. Guilt, an unfamiliar feeling, flooded him. *What the hell am I doing here?* He was drawn to the mother, drawn to the child. The feeling was far, far stronger than he'd expected.

He imagined Dany's sweet, supple body under his, her long legs wrapped around him, her sweet-smelling hair soft against his lips. Her heart's blood beating in her slender throat. He wanted her. Badly.

Tonight, for some reason, she seemed less vulnerable than she'd been the night before, perhaps because they were on her turf. She was fair game. But what about the child? Dany had warned him off Sarah in no uncertain terms, and she was right to do so. The little girl had no defenses, and only a wretch would come on to her like Daddy when all he really wanted was a few hours in Mommy's bed.

Rambler wandered back into the dining room and looked down at the setup for Hunt the Night City. He was amazed at the intensity with which he'd been rolling the dice. It was an adolescent fantasy game, for God's sake. Why had he gotten so caught up in such foolishness?

Max put the pieces away and folded up the board. He considered letting himself out and leaving Dany in peace, but couldn't quite bring himself to do it. Not yet. His thirst for her was too strong to be denied.

When she rejoined him fifteen minutes later, Dany was surprised to find all the game pieces back in their box. "Don't you want to play anymore?" she asked. "You were on a hot streak."

"That's okay. I think you've got the hang of it now. How's Sarah?"

"Asleep. I'm a little worried about her. She's had nightmares on and off ever since her father left. She never used to have trouble sleeping when we were still a family."

Don't even ask, Max told himself. The last thing you need is to listen to her life history. But he asked anyway: "What went wrong between you and your husband, Dany?"

She shrugged. "We married too young, I suppose. Greg wasn't ready for the responsibilities of a family. He was never home; too wrapped up in his career as a rising corporate executive. In the end, he just left."

"With another woman?"

She nodded. "He married her as soon as the divorce became final."

"Ah."

She raised her eyebrows. "If you think I'm still mourning his betrayal, you're wrong. I don't miss Greg. Things had been going wrong between us for some time. But Sarah misses him. He wasn't even a caring father to her, and yet she worships him."

"He's Daddy. It's natural for a kid to adore Daddy, even if the guy's a creep."

"I'm just sorry I couldn't give her a daddy who was worthy of her love. In that respect, I feel I've failed her."

"She's got a wonderful mommy. That's more than some children have."

She smiled at him. He needn't have said that, but it made her feel good that he had. He spoke as if he really meant it, too, which was nice. It occurred to her that she was beginning to like Max Rambler. More, much more than she'd intended.

He stayed for another hour, sitting beside her on the living room sofa while she talked about her marriage, her job, even her childhood. He was easy to talk to, a good listener. She didn't notice until he was getting ready to leave that he'd told her little in return about himself. He had a subtle way of turning aside personal questions, seeming to give an answer but saying nothing of any real consequence. She'd heard more about him from Cass than she'd heard from his own lips.

He made no move to touch her until she saw him to the door. There, in the hallway, he took her hand, stroking her wrist with his elegant, sensitive fingers. She looked into his eyes and read his intention burning in their emerald depths.

"I want to kiss you, Dany. A proper kiss, that is. Not like last night. Not one given as if you're in fear for your life."

Dany smiled, but she hesitated. She remembered the terror he'd induced in her the previous night with the vampire's kiss. Even then she'd been attracted to him, to those beguiling eyes, that long, lean body. Even when she'd thought him dangerous, she'd felt his pull.

A different kind of danger was beating between them now. *Don't even consider it.* A sexual infatuation with Max Rambler would cause nothing but trouble. She had already expressed her worries about Sarah; beyond that, there was the complication of her job. She was new in Chesterton and still on probation. The St. Crispin's community was small, and it would be difficult to keep her private life private. No doubt she was supposed to set a moral example to her students; an example that could hardly be maintained if she flung herself into a passionate entanglement with a virile charmer like Max.

Say no. Smile politely and send him on his way.

"Dany?"

Damn! He was so lanky and tall, his hair was so fragrant and his eyes so deliciously green. Physically, he was exactly the type of man she liked best. It had been ages since she'd met anyone who appealed to her. Anyway, what harm could one kiss do?

"I can't stand the suspense, Dany. Are you going to kiss me or not?"

She grinned, seized by an impulse to get back at him for all his teasing. "Only if you'll allow me to perform a little test on you first."

"Can't be too careful nowadays, huh? What sort of test?"

She took his arm and drew him toward a marble-topped table. Above it was hanging a gilt-edged mirror. "You'll have to admit you're pretty strange, Max. You sleep during the day, you enter through windows, you won't eat or drink." She'd offered him a cup of coffee while they'd been playing Hunt the Night City, but he'd refused. "I didn't see any mirrors last night in your place. You won't mind, I'm sure, if I check to make sure you reflect before I allow your fangs anywhere near my throat."

She expected him to laugh, but instead his mouth tightened. For a second she thought he was going to refuse to enter the area reflected by the mirror.

"Fine," he said at last. "Reassure yourself."

She felt a prickle at the back of her neck as her superstitious streak acted up once again. What if he didn't reflect? What would he do to her if her test confirmed that he really was one of the undead?

"Losing your nerve, Dany? Here." He slung an arm around her shoulders and moved with her to the edge of the table. He pulled her close so their heads were together, black hair and copper, the respective colors mingling where their scalps touched. Sure enough, his face was there in the mirror, darkly handsome, his sensual lips curling as his eyes met hers.

Dany felt a stab of real, unqualified relief. But almost immediately thereafter she mocked herself for believing there could be anything supernatural about this man.

"So much for your test. No—" he stopped her as she was about to pull away "—keep watching our reflections." He glided his fingers into her hair, pulling gently at her chignon until it began to come loose. "I want you to see how delicious you look to me, and how erotic we look together."

Then he opened his palm under her chin, lifted her face and kissed her.

Sensual heat exploded in Dany at the sight of his mouth claiming hers. She saw it, and felt it, too. His lips were warm, lush, sensitive; her own looked fluttery and vulnerable as he crushed them beneath his.

The hand under her chin dropped to her shoulder, then moved up and down her arm in a feather-light caress. His other hand wound more deeply into her hair, pulling it down in masses of copper profusion about her shoulders. His body was strong and firm against hers. Without hurting her, he let his dominance be felt, holding her in such a way that she couldn't move. Not that she wanted to. Willingly, she gave herself up to the seduction of his mouth, his hands, his tongue.

"Open your mouth," he ordered. "That's it, perfect. Yes." He stroked the surfaces of her teeth with his tongue, then delved behind them to touch her own tongue so erotically that she sighed and wrapped her arms around him, drawing him even closer. His shoulders were sinewy and strong; she could feel his muscles bunching and relaxing under her hands as she passionately returned his kiss. Colors seemed to flash behind her eyelids, and she began to see lush, sensual images of bare bodies moving together, coupling, twisting, pirouetting in a sensual ballet. She wasn't sure where the images were coming from . . . his mind, perhaps. They seemed too vividly masculine to be her own.

His or hers, the thoughts electrified her. She dragged at the fabric of his sweater as the need built to touch his naked flesh. She pictured herself being stripped of her clothing by the knowing hands that were already moving on her body, exploring her throat, her breasts, the curve of her hip. She saw them in bed together, loving each other eagerly, hard.

She knew she was losing control. If she didn't pull away from him now, it would happen. Incredible though it seemed, she was on the verge of surrender. She scrambled for willpower, for restraint. *You must stop him now.* Turning her head to one side, Dany freed her mouth long enough to say, "The deal was for a kiss, Max. Nothing more."

She felt him exhale. There was something about that long in-out burden of his breath that touched her deeply. Slowly he raised his head and loosened his grip on her hair. His other hand still toyed with the material at the V of her sweater. He was giving her that winsome smile again, but the expression in his eyes was enigmatic.

"It's delicate and rare, this feeling between us, Dany. I'm aching to make love to you. Why not invite me into your bedroom and take a chance on me?"

She pulled away from him, her cheeks hot. "I'm sorry, Max. I'd really rather not."

He shook his head regretfully and stroked her cheek with his thumb. Good for you, Dany, a low voice inside him said. Stop me. I'll hurt you, and your daughter too, if you don't.

He banished the thought. The last thing he needed now was a conscience. "D'you blame me for trying?"

She smiled. "Of course not."

"You know I'll try again."

She shivered. It sounded a bit like a threat.

He released her abruptly and went to the door. Dany watching him, trying to gauge his mood and the somber expression on his face. Had she offended him? It didn't occur to her that he might be torn within himself.

When he turned on the threshold to say goodbye, he was wearing that mischievous smile again. "Maybe it's just as well. You probably wouldn't enjoy bedding down in my coffin. Most women don't."

Dany laughed. His dry sense of humor appealed to her. Everything about him appealed to her, blast him.

"I'll see you tomorrow night at eight-thirty."

"Well after sunset," she noted with a smile.

Those laugh lines of his deepened. "Which reminds me, there's something I ought to tell you. A confession of sorts."

"What?"

"I misled you about the mirror, I'm afraid. It's not true that a vampire has no reflection. Another myth, Dany my love. Vampires are flesh and blood, just like humans. I assure you, they reflect."

She stared at him, blinking. At least he hadn't said *we reflect*.

"Forget most of the things you think you know about vampires, Dany. I'll teach you the facts."

"Max—"

"Good night, Headmistress," he added, laughing. He moved down her front walk and vanished into the night.

Six

——

Dany stood on her front walk the following evening with her hands thrust deep into the pockets of her cashmere jacket. She looked up and down the quiet lane. No sign of him. Max Rambler had said he'd meet her here at eight-thirty, but it was twenty to nine and he hadn't shown up yet. She hoped he'd hurry. The air was cold and it felt as if there might be a storm brewing. In the mountains, it wasn't too early for snow.

"Surely you're not going vampire hunting dressed like that," said a voice so close to her ear that she couldn't contain a gasp. Max was there, just beside her, tall and knife-slender. Dressed in his usual dark clothing, he melted into the night. She hadn't seen or heard him until he was upon her. "Evening, Headmistress," he added, shooting her his devastating smile. "Sorry I'm late."

"Hi, Max. What's wrong with the way I'm dressed?" She cast a glance down over her wool skirt and fine leather boots. She had dressed to be warm, but she'd also taken special pains with her appearance. During the day she had to be so careful to dress down that she rarely wore more than a smidgen of makeup. This evening, though, she had put in a long session with her hot comb, eyeliner, lipliner and mascara, making every effort to produce just the right chic result.

Rambler fingered the lapel of her camel-toned jacket. "Too light in color; you stand out. And far too fine in fabric for what we're going to be doing tonight. Haven't you got a pair of jeans and a dark jacket? Your boots are gorgeous—sexy as hell, by the way—but hardly appropriate for the task at hand. What if we have to run? Those high heels will trip you."

Dany bit back a sigh. "I can change."

"Let's go," he said, taking her arm and walking back up the walk to her house.

"Where's your car?"

"Didn't bring it. I walked down."

"You walked all the way down from your mountain?"

"It's only a couple of miles. Seems like longer because the road's so terrible. Besides, there's a path through the woods that leads directly to the St. Crispin's campus, and hiking's a hobby of mine."

"But it's pitch-dark outside, Max."

"We undeads have remarkable night vision."

"Oh God. Don't start that again."

He grinned. "Don't fret. I've already drunk my nightly ration of blood, so you're safe with me."

"You just won't let up, will you?"

"I'm incorrigible," he agreed. "When your eyes go all soft and skittish and you get this adorable little crease in your brow, I'm seized with an irresistible desire to tease you."

"So I've gathered!"

With one hand under her arm, he urged her up the steps to her darkened porch. For a moment they stood there in front of her door, and Dany felt his breath stirring the hair just alongside her ear. He wasn't embracing her, but she knew he was contemplating it. Hastily she reached for the switch that turned on the overhead light.

Max blinked. He had mascara-thick lashes that blurred like soot against his pale skin. His rueful smile did not accord very well with the hint of danger in his eyes. "That's it, Headmistress. Kill the mood."

"You were about to grab me. Right here on my front porch."

He shrugged and gave a sigh. "Guilty as charged."

"I'm not going traipsing around the campus all evening with you if you're going to be grabbing me every chance you get."

"Not too smooth, am I?" For an instant he looked wistful, giving her another of those surprising hints of his vulnerability. His sexual aggressiveness was undeniably exciting, but it was this occasional glimpse of inner uncertainty that really endeared him to her.

"Shall I wait outside? You said something about keeping me away from your daughter."

Which made her feel like a heel. "Don't be silly." Spontaneously, she grabbed his hand and led him into her house.

Sarah recognized him at once and came running. She was wearing her nightgown and slippers and she had her puppy under one arm. "Hi, Max!"

He gave her a hug. "Hi, sweetie. Why aren't you in bed?"

"I was, but I sneaked downstairs when I heard you and my mommy talking on the front walk."

Max caught Dany's eye and grinned ruefully. "Did we wake you up?"

"Oh no, I was awake. I stay up very late, you know."

Jennifer, her baby-sitter, looking embarrassed, put in, "I'm sorry, Ms. Holland. I didn't know she was still awake until I heard her footsteps on the stairs."

"That's okay, Jennifer. This is a friend of mine, Mr. Rambler. Why don't you talk to him for a few minutes while I take Sarah back upstairs?"

Jennifer was staring at Max with round, startled eyes that indicated that she knew very well who he was. David Ellis had probably told her he was a vampire. "That's okay," she said. "I'll get her back in bed for you, don't worry. C'mon, Sarah." She had to pry the little girl away from Max. "I'll read you another story."

Max watched, frowning, as the teenager fled up the stairs. "I seem to have frightened your baby-sitter without even trying."

"She's one of David Ellis's friends. No doubt she's heard about your alleged penchant for sucking blood."

"I'd like to meet this David Ellis," Max said in an ominous tone. "I think he and I are due for a little chat."

She touched his arm. "I don't blame you. Sit down. I'll throw on some jeans and be right back."

Dany ran upstairs to her bedroom and regretfully removed the designer clothing. She changed into jeans and a sweater and donned a pair of old sneakers. After a quick look in the mirror, she decided to change her earrings, too; she didn't want the gold hoops she was wearing to pull out of her ears and get lost. "So much for glamour," she sighed as she surveyed her new reflection in the mirror. She left the painstaking makeup job alone. She still had *some* vanity.

She went in to kiss her daughter, then hurried back downstairs to Max, who slipped his hand into hers and treated her to the full force of his appraising stare. "Your new costume's much more appropriate, if not as seductive as the first. Got a flashlight? Where we're going, we'll need one."

She nodded, showing him the flashlight in the pocket of her jacket. "Where are we going?"

"To hunt the night city and see what we find."

"Where are you taking me?" she repeated a little later as she followed him across the lacrosse field toward the sports center. It was an old building, housing a swimming pool, a gym and girls' and boys' locker rooms. Max moved swiftly, and Dany found it difficult to keep up with him. He seemed to glide over the ground, so long was his stride. She was left to trot along in his wake. After a few minutes of this she had a stitch in her side, but she didn't like to complain. I've got to start jogging or something, she told herself wryly.

Max stopped near the edge of the tennis courts and waited for her to catch up. "There's an entrance to the tunnels in the basement of the gym."

"What tunnels?"

"Do you mean to tell me you, the headmistress, don't know about the network of tunnels under the school?"

Dany shook her head. "This is the first I've heard of them. What sort of tunnels are they?"

"Ventilation and heating, mostly. They house the school's electrical system, too. They're big, high enough to stand in, and they used to be considered quite dangerous. When I was a student here a kid got trapped down there, broke his leg and nearly died of exposure before somebody found him and pulled him out."

"Why would anybody want to go down into a network of ventilation tunnels?"

"Can't you guess? They're dark and mysterious and they meander underneath the campus like an enormous maze. It's a perfect place to play the game. The tunnels are good for other things, too, like illicit drinking and sexual activity," he added with a sidelong glance at her. "The things St. Crispin's is so careful to restrict above the ground."

"Great," she muttered. My God, she'd been so scrupulous about enforcing Edith Kenworthy's rules, even though she herself had been dubious about their efficacy. So far, at least, she couldn't deny she'd been impressed with the results. Her students were well-mannered teenagers who seemed to have more respect for authority than any she'd encountered in her previous jobs. There was no evidence of alcohol or drugs on campus. Only one girl had become pregnant in the course of the past year. St. Crispin's had struck her as a remarkably innocent place.

But now she'd begun to wonder if she'd been conned all these months by a bunch of clever, savvy teenage brats.

"Got the keys to the gym?" Max asked when they found the building locked.

Wordlessly, she handed him her ring of master keys. Max got the door open and ushered her into the dark. "Let's leave the lights off. We don't want to advertise our presence. Where's your flashlight? Turn it on."

While she struggled to do so, off he went, leading the way to the basement of the gym without seeming to require any light himself.

The air was stale in the basement, suggesting that nobody had been down there for some time. The thought crossed her mind that if David was right and Max was some kind of nut with violent intentions toward her, she was completely at his mercy. If anything happened to her, nobody would think of looking for her here.

"You're sure it's been twenty years since you were last down here? You seem to know your way around."

"Good memory. I'm afraid I was one of the ringleaders of the tunnel brigade back in those days."

"If it was so forbidden and dangerous, that makes you a reckless troublemaker of a student."

"Reckless, maybe, but I wasn't a troublemaker. Not on a regular basis, anyway. I was too shy to be a trouble-maker."

"Ah, yes. Shy."

He turned his head to look back at her. "I still don't strike you as shy?"

She started to say no, then thought better of it. Maybe shyness could account for that disarming vulnerability of his.

"Well, I am," he insisted. "Why do you think I'm such a recluse? I'm okay one-on-one, I suppose, but get me into a group and I clam up completely. I'm not very sociable."

"A lot of people feel the same way," she said lightly.

The entrance to the tunnels was through a metal grille about four feet high. As Max wrestled the grille off the hole in the wall that it covered, Dany shone her flashlight into the yawning blackness. The passage was narrow and long, stretching away far beyond the flashlight's beam. There was a distinct musty odor emanating from within.

She drew back, uneasy. "I thought you said these things were high enough to stand in."

"They are, in most areas. Don't be misled by the size of the grill, it doesn't correspond to the diameter of the tunnel."

With a bow and a flourish, he pulled the grille aside for her to enter. "After you, Headmistress."

She hesitated, unable to repress a nasty little image of him closing the grill, jamming it securely back into the wall and abandoning her. Her colorful imagination again. "I don't know, Max. What's the point of this, exactly? I mean, if it's really so dangerous..."

"Wimp," he said softly.

She lifted her chin. "I'm too old to play chicken."

"We're not playing chicken. We're playing Hunt the Night City." He squeezed her hand briefly. "Don't worry,

Dany. Nothing terrible's going to happen to you in there, I promise.''

"What about the electrical cables you mentioned? I wouldn't want to be fooling around with any of those.''

"They're strung high, flush with the ceiling. Anyway, they're insulated. Even if you touch one you won't get a shock.''

She sighed, out of excuses. "I must be crazy," she muttered as she ducked into the hole. She shone the flashlight ahead of her, seeing that the passageway did indeed spread out on all sides. The ceiling, which appeared to be constructed of some sort of corrugated metal piping, arched a few inches over her head. She saw the cables. They were wrapped in thick rubber.

Inside the tunnel system the air was hot and humid, and her flashlight did little to relieve the absolute darkness of the place. "I can't believe I'm doing this. Are you coming?" There was a metallic clang behind her as the grille fell back into place. Dany's voice rose in pitch as she added, "Where are you, Rambler?"

She jumped at the feel of his hand riding the small of her back. "I'm right here, just behind you. I was just replacing the grid." She heard a bumping sound, and the walls around them vibrated. Max cursed loudly. "Correction: the tunnels are high enough for a teenager to stand in. I guess I've grown a bit since then." He took the flashlight and checked the place out. "You're not claustrophobic, I hope."

"I never have been, but I've never done anything like this. Are you?"

"Naw. Sleeping in a coffin all day cures you of that pretty fast. Ow! What was that?"

"My elbow, Drac. Stop teasing me."

"Felt like a stake aimed at my heart."

"What's that unpleasant smell?" she asked as they advanced a few paces down the tunnel.

"God knows. Mold, probably. There used to be places where yucky green stuff would grow all over the walls. You'll find little puddles of condensed water here and there, too. Not to mention an occasional rat."

"Rats? I hate rats."

His arm slipped around her shoulders. "Relax. I promise to slay any rat that ventures to attack us, no matter how vicious the critter might be." He stopped short. "Wait a sec." His voice lowered to a whisper. "I think I hear something."

Dany listened. She didn't hear a thing. "What?"

"Shh."

Still nothing.

"Footsteps. Voices," said Max. "Coming from one of the main tunnels ahead."

"Your senses are obviously more acute than mine. I can't hear it."

He was moving again, going forward in that quick, silent manner of his. "There's a turnoff nearby, if my memory serves me well. In fact, there are several turnoffs. This place is a real maze. You might take note, if you will, of the turns we make. I have a pretty good sense of direction, but I'm not infallible. We wouldn't want to get lost down here, would we?"

No, she thought as her foot slipped on a patch of the infamous green mold. We certainly wouldn't.

"Here," he said, stopping so suddenly she collided with his body. He shut off the flashlight, leaving them in impenetrable darkness. For a couple of seconds her stomach was pressed against his buttocks. He felt very nice, taut and muscular. He had the kind of build that made her toes tingle. But even so, she wouldn't have stayed so close to him if she hadn't been afraid to move so much as an inch in the dark.

"I don't want anybody to see our light," he said quietly. "The tunnel under the gym ends here. Can you feel the change in the air currents? We're about to enter one of the cross tunnels. It goes under the playing field and on toward the main buildings of the campus. Listen. Can you hear them now?"

In the distance, Dany caught the timbre of a female voice. There was silence for a moment, then a male voice answered. She couldn't make out what they were saying, but they sounded excited. "I don't see any lights," she whispered.

"No." He continued to listen in silence, his head cocked slightly to one side. The voices faded. "They've turned off," he said at last. "They've probably entered one of the tunnels that run parallel to this one."

"How many tunnels are there?"

"Dozens. Maybe hundreds. There should be a map somewhere. The people who maintain the heating plant must have a map."

"But Max, what exactly is this network of tunnels for? It can't be ventilation, not completely. And electric wires could have been strung above the ground. When were they constructed, and why?"

"I don't know for sure, but the story I've heard most often is that they were built during World War II. St. Crispin's was used as an army training camp during the summer of 1944. You know the military—they do the damnedest things. Probably built the tunnels as a place to hide military secrets if Hitler invaded." He was advancing once again. "Come on, our quarry's getting away."

Dany followed him down another long passageway, around a sharp bend, into a zigzag and up what felt like a hill. They made a right turn into a narrower tunnel that had even less headroom than the others. This time even she had to slouch, and poor Max was stooped over. It was hot underground; she was soon sweating. Once a small pipe blew off a jet of steam right in front of her face, causing her to yelp and leap back. Max grabbed her as she stumbled. "I forgot to warn you about those steam pressure valves. You have to be careful; they can burn you. Are you okay?"

"I think so, yes."

They made a sharp left, hiked through the darkness for what seemed like forever, then came at last into a small round chamber. "Aha," said Max. He played the flashlight around, casting weird shadows on the walls. "Here's some evidence for you. They *are* playing the game down here, Dany. Look. The sarcophagi of the undead."

The light revealed several oblong boxes neatly arranged in a row on the floor. They were painted with arcane signs and symbols, and they looked unpleasantly like coffins. Max stepped over to one and shone the light on its surface. Dany could feel herself shivering. "You're not going to open it, are you?"

"Why not? Vampires arise at sunset. At this time of night it's sure to be empty."

Dany's laugh sounded high and nervous. "I don't like this, Max. It's one thing to play Hunt the Night City at the dining table, imagining underground tunnels and chambers and such, but to actually recreate them . . . Oh God, don't open it. Stop. What if there's a body in there, or—"

"Take it easy, Dany. It's a cardboard box, painted with poster paint. A prop, nothing more. See?" He dislodged the cover of the sarcophagus. "No body, no vampire."

A prop. "David Ellis belongs to the drama club. Maybe some of the other kids from that group play Hunt the Night City, too."

"Very likely."

Gingerly, she peered into the empty casket. "Ugh. Empty or not, it still gives me the creeps."

"If they have access to props and scenery, I wonder if they've rigged up the other rooms somewhere, too. The golden tower, for instance, or the dungeon."

"Oh no, you're not dragging me to the dungeon, Rambler. Enough is enough. Why don't we think about turning back?"

Max aimed the beam of light in her direction. She turned her face away, embarrassed. She was sweaty. Her makeup was probably streaking down her cheeks, and as for her hair, the humidity in the tunnels had made it curl damply around her face. "You look like hell," he said cheerfully. "You've got huge black circles under your eyes."

"My mascara's running, thank you very much."

"Rule number one, never wear mascara when you're traveling underground."

"Would have been nice if you'd told me the rules before you lured me into the catacombs."

"Want to hear rule number two?"

"I don't think so."

His voice had turned husky, and Dany retreated a step. Uh-oh. Maybe smeared mascara turned him on.

The beam moved again, more slowly this time. From hair to lips to throat to breasts, the amber beam poured over her like a caress. Something about the ruthlessness of that light unnerved her. Here in the heavy darkness there was no escaping it, no escaping him.

Without thinking, Dany reached out and snatched the flashlight from his hand. Max moved his arm reflexively just as she touched him, and somehow the light slipped through her fingers, clattered to the floor, winked once and died.

As the shadows closed around them Max muttered a word that was not normally heard within—or under—the hallowed halls of St. Crispin's. "Oh my God," Dany echoed, appalled at her carelessness. "Is it broken?"

Max stooped. She heard him recover the flashlight; she heard him click its switch. The tunnel remained absolutely dark. "Looks that way. Got another one, darlin'?"

"No, of course not!"

"Rule number two is, don't drop the flashlight in the maze. Particularly when you aren't carrying a spare."

Dany repeated Max's salty term, then went on to embroider fiercely upon the same theme, causing him to laugh softly and say, "If only the trustees could hear you now. Shame on you, Headmistress."

"Max, I'm so sorry. What are we going to do? We'll never find our way out of here without light."

"I don't know. We could grope our way along, I suppose. Have you been keeping track of the turns we made?"

"Yes. It was two rights, a left and a right." She thought a minute. "Or was it two rights, a left and a left?"

"Great, Dany."

"You said you had an excellent sense of direction." Her voice took on a minor note of panic. "You claimed to know your way around these tunnels. If you've lost us down here, Max Rambler, I'll strangle you."

"Take it easy. We're not lost."

She couldn't see him, but she felt him come up against her. His arms slid around her waist, and the palms of his hands pressed the seat of her jeans in an outrageously familiar manner.

"I'll get you out, I promise," he continued, his voice low and silky. "But it's going to cost you. There's a stiff penalty for breaking the flashlight, I'm afraid."

"We're trapped in a maze, Rambler. This is hardly the time to wax amorous."

Although she tried to sound discouraging, Dany's cheeks were hot and little sparks of excitement were zipping along her nerves. He was cloaked in night, and there was something stunningly erotic about not being able to see him. She had a clear mental image of his well-cut features, his sensual lower lip, his deep-set green eyes, which were always dancing, burning.

She was blinded by the night, but her other senses had come more sharply alive. She heard the rustling of his fingers in her hair, the slight creak of his leather jacket as he drew her more firmly into his embrace. She smelled the faint salty musk of his skin. An ache spread through the pit of her stomach, sending hot flashes up into her breasts. Her nipples tautened, and she pressed herself against him. It seemed incredible, given their predicament, but she very much wanted to sink down on the floor and make love.

"I'd prefer a bed," he whispered, performing his uncanny mind-reading trick again.

"No beds in here," she said shakily. "I don't know about you, but I don't consider a sarcophagus a bed."

He laughed softly. "I'll make a deal with you, Dany. I'll get you out of here if in return you—"

"No," she interrupted. "You got me into this and you're obliged to get me out. I don't owe you anything."

He didn't argue. He simply bent his head and kissed her, swiftly, masterfully, hard. By the time he lifted his mouth from hers, she was weak-kneed and trembling with passion. She didn't think she would have been able to continue standing if he hadn't supported her, his lanky body rock-solid, steady, and deliciously aroused.

Dany felt a wild and joyous recklessness come over her. She'd been at St. Crispin's for six months, and during that entire time she'd lived an exemplary life. She'd been ladylike, proper, well disciplined, conservative in speech, dress and behavior. Indeed, she'd been too overwhelmed by the former headmistress's sterling reputation to be anything else.

But this wasn't her real personality. The real Dany loved bright colors, laughter, sensual delights. The real Dany

adored the unusual and pored over tales of terror and romance. And the real Dany hadn't fallen wildly, passionately, devil-may-care in love with anybody in far too long a
time.

Max Rambler was perfect for her. He was just weird
enough to appeal to her sense of the absurd. He was clever,
he was humorous, and he was more sensitive than he let on.
She liked him. And his body... well, she loved that.

She leaned back in his arms, wishing she could see his
face. "Okay," she whispered. "I owe you. Get us out and
I'm yours."

"You mean that?" He sounded astonished. "Really,
Dany?"

"Yes, really. I may end up regretting it, but..." She let
the words trail off. "You have to rescue us first, Drac, so I
hope your remarkable night vision's in good working order."

"Oh, I assure you it is. Promise me, Dany." His hands
were heavy on her shoulders. "Promise me you won't re-
nege on this as soon as you're safely out of the tunnels."

"For God's sake, Max!"

"Promise."

"All right, I promise. You have my word."

He kissed her again, and Dany could feel the smile on his
lips. "I'll have us at the door to your bedroom in under ten
minutes."

"God, you're cocky. How?"

He turned her loose long enough to reach into the pocket
of his jacket. She heard a click, then the chamber was
flooded with light. "You may be careless," he said smugly,
"but I always carry a spare."

With the aid of the new flashlight and his excellent sense
of direction, Max led Dany down a tunnel she didn't think
they'd been in before, around several bends, through a

puddle that wet her sneakers and set her cursing and finally up a metal ladder. At the top they were confronted with another circular grille. "Where are we?" she asked as he dismantled it.

"You'll see in a minute. This comes off easily," he added, referring to the grille. "Kids must be going in and out of here all the time." He climbed through the opening and reached back to give her a hand.

"You know what I think? I think you've been down here more recently than twenty years ago."

"Suspicious, aren't you?"

"After what you just pulled with the flashlight, yes. I should have known you couldn't be trusted. I should have known you'd cheat."

He was standing upright in some sort of cellar now, holding the grille open for her. He made as if to shut it just as she was starting to climb through. "You wouldn't be thinking of going back on your word, would you?"

"You tricked me, Max!" She deliberately exaggerated her annoyance. "Let me out."

"A promise is a promise, Danielle."

She liked the way he said her full name. His voice caressed the syllables. Desire stabbed through her again. In the dim light of a dusty cellar—she wasn't sure yet in what building they had emerged—Max looked incredibly enticing. Like hers, his dark hair was curling from the humidity in the tunnels, and there was something about his rather grimy face that touched her. Behind the easy male arrogance, behind the trick he'd used to trap her, Dany knew he was afraid she'd change her mind.

Drop-dead handsome though he was, Rambler was no swinging sexual athlete, she sensed. Far from being casual about his conquest, he was overjoyed at the idea that she might really go to bed with him. And he'd be crushed if she turned around now and declared she would not.

"Don't worry, Max," she said lightly. "I don't go back on my promises, even if they are extracted by deceit."

He grinned and held the grille wide so she could clamber out.

They were in the basement of the library. Dany recognized the place as Max led her through a doorway into the stacks. He had chosen their exit well; the library was a good deal closer to her house than the gym.

The building was closed for the evening, so Dany unlocked one of the side doors and let them out into the night. It was a short walk back to her place. When they reached the low hedge that separated the headmistress's cottage from the eastern edge of the campus, Max's hand cupped her arm. The contact sent a tongue of fire racing through her. "Shall I wait outside while you take care of the baby-sitter?"

"Yes, please. I'd like to be as discreet as possible about this."

"One advantage of loving a creature of the night—we can disappear at will, thus protecting our beloved's reputation."

"I don't want Sarah to see you, either, if by any chance she's up."

"Yes, I know," he said more seriously. "Don't worry; we'll be careful."

"It's just that there's been no one for me since Greg and I split up, and I'm not sure how she'd take it."

"If she's awake I won't come in," he said without rancor. He caught her wrist as she was about to move away. "But don't lie to me. Don't use your daughter as an excuse to hold me off. I'll know if you lie, Dany."

"I don't lie," she said a little stiffly.

His fingers slowly uncurled from her wrist. "Okay. Go on. I'll be waiting."

Dany's insides were churning with combined desire and nervous tension as she unlocked her front door, greeted

Jennifer and ran upstairs to check on Sarah. The child was deeply asleep. Dany kissed her and firmly shut her bedroom door. No excuse there.

She paid Jennifer and offered to see her safely to her dorm. As they walked out into the lane, Dany noticed her glancing apprehensively around, as if afraid she might see Ms. Holland's infamous vampire companion. But, as promised, Max had disappeared.

He reappeared to hover over her when Dany returned to the front porch and slipped her key into the door. She could feel him, tall and strong and outrageously masculine beside her.

"Your daughter's asleep?"

She nodded.

"Good."

They entered the house. She closed the door. As she turned to face him, he advanced a step, crowding her back against the wall. The naked desire showing in his face was far stronger than anything he'd revealed to her before. It altered the cast of his features, making him appear harsh and predatory.

Wait, wait. What am I doing? Her hands flew up to ward him off, but it was already too late. Her fingers encountered the solid flesh-and-bone structure of his shoulders, and then his mouth was on her throat.

"You won't be sorry," he murmured, his breath fire-hot against her skin. "Whatever happens, I'll make sure you're not sorry."

She shivered as his lips nibbled her, for there was still a portion of her brain that half expected to feel the sharp driving pressure of his teeth. If he was a creature of darkness, she was lost. She ached for him, yearned for him; there was no way she would ever be able to resist the demonic kiss.

"There's something I've always wondered," she whispered as his lips fluttered over her cheeks, her eyelids, the corners of her mouth.

"Mmm?" He touched what was left of the smudged mascara, then, tenderly, kissed it away. "What, pretty lady?"

"Is it possible for vampires to make love? In the usual manner, I mean?"

"Point me to your bedroom and we'll find out."

Seven

—

Max proved to possess all the smooth and dashing qualities of the most delicious romantic hero. He swept Dany into his arms and carried her up the stairway that led to the starlit room where she slept. "You'll drop me," she protested.

"No. Never. You're light as an elfin creature, my darling copper-haired love."

He shouldered his way into her bedroom and laid her down in the middle of her chintz-covered single bed. He sat down beside her, stroking her hair. She couldn't help but be aware of the way his dynamic presence filled the room. Her furniture was delicate, feminine, but he was tough, strong and totally male. "I guess you don't entertain a lot of night visitors. Your bed is almost as narrow as my coffin."

"You should feel right at home, then."

He brushed his fingers across her lips, a maddening kind of teasing that turned her anticipation up another notch. "I hope you know what you're doing, Dany. This will be a claiming. After tonight, there'll be no looking back."

She swallowed, riveted by the leashed sense of purpose she felt emanating from him. No man had ever put it to her in such a straightforward, primitive manner. "A claiming?"

His fingers skated provocatively over her shoulders and down her arms. "Yes." He rubbed his palms against her breasts, which started an even more insistent ache in the pit of her stomach. She squirmed a little, ever more conscious of her own melting heat. "I'm your destiny, Danielle."

"I think you're the last of the great romantics, Mr. Rambler." She reached up and cupped his jaw. His chin was rough from the growth of his whiskers. She rubbed a smidgen of grime from the end of his nose. "Look at you. Look at both of us—all grubby from crawling around in the tunnels. D'you want to take a shower together first?"

He looked both surprised and pleased. "You'd take a shower with me?"

"Why not? I'm about to do a whole lot more with you than that!"

"Guess I'm still a shy boy at heart."

"Oh, well, I'm not shy." She sat up and offered him her hand. "Come on. Bathroom's through here."

Under the soft lights of the bathroom, Dany turned on the shower and began to undress. But after having kicked off her shoes and pulled her sweater over her head, she discovered that Max was still standing there, staring, in no apparent hurry to shed his own clothes. She blushed. Was she being too uninhibited for his liking? What if he thought her a brazen, shameless hussy? "Is something wrong?"

He shook his head slowly, then smiled. "No, love. I don't want to miss anything, that's all. You're very sweet, very natural. Other women might play a lot of silly games, but that's not your way, is it?"

"You're the expert on games, not me."

He stepped close enough to touch her. She was wearing a blouse that fastened with small pearl buttons down the front. "Let me help with this part, okay?"

With great dexterity he dealt with the buttons, then opened her blouse and pushed it to the sides. His gaze seemed to burn through the fragile silk and lace that still covered her breasts. She felt her nipples harden. The mere thought of his touching her made them ache and swell.

"You're so pretty." He jerked the blouse from her arms and tossed it on the floor. His fingers slipped around behind her back and unhooked her bra, then that, too, haphazardly followed the blouse. With exquisite care, he touched her breasts with the tips of his fingers. Dany made a sound in the back of her throat. "So pretty," he repeated, his voice rough-edged with arousal. "So soft."

Dany swayed against him. My legs are like straws, she thought wryly. She began tearing at his buttons. Her brain was filled with erotic images, picture after picture of dreamy-eyed lovers engaged in passionate sexual embraces. He's doing this, she thought vaguely. He's sending these images to me.

Within a few seconds they were naked together, two slender bodies, one lean and hard, the other smaller, more delicately curved. Max's skin was pale and smooth, not hairy at all except for the glossy, dark mat that spread across his chest, then arrowed down over his flat belly. His muscles were spare but well defined, giving him the grace and elegance of a dancer. He had a trim waist and narrow hips, and his legs extended forever.

"Do I pass muster?" He was grinning at her all-too-obvious appraisal.

"I'll say."

"So do you. You're lovely all over, Dany." His eyes caressed her. "I've never seen a woman I wanted more."

She felt the same about him. The steam from the hot shower was fogging the air around them, making him look almost ethereal, as if it weren't entirely clear where the boundaries of his flesh were. Once again she thought there must be something supernatural about him, for his form was almost too perfect, and he was almost too much the man of her dreams. But when he pulled her close and held her, she knew he was real. She could feel his bones, his sinews, the heated pounding of his blood. Against the muscles of her stomach she could feel the root of his manhood, throbbing with his life force. He fit so snugly against her. The symmetry of their bodies made them seem an already-mated pair.

He lowered his head and kissed her mouth. She clung to him, drowning in erotic sensation. As their tongues touched, little shivers chased each other up and down her spine. He drew back, making his kisses small, teasing, too-shallow nips, and she arched against him, straining for more. They battled briefly for control of the kiss. Smiling wickedly, Max captured her face between his palms and held her still so he could plunder her mouth with his tongue. Dany yielded. She was beside herself; she couldn't remember ever having felt so aroused.

"The shower, Dany."

"Oh, yes, I nearly forgot!"

The shower seemed to her to be one of the most refined instruments of torture ever invented, for it forced them to touch each other all over, producing constantly escalated levels of excitement without granting any relief. Dany heard herself moan in the most wanton way imaginable as he wet a washcloth, soaped it up and ran the slightly rough fabric over her breasts, her belly, and down to the tangled red-gold curls between her legs. Every time he touched her, he murmured endearments and praise, making her feel like the most beautiful, most desirable woman in the world.

PLAY
SILHOUETTE'S

LUCKY HEARTS
GAME

AND YOU COULD GET

★ FREE BOOKS
★ A FREE UMBRELLA
★ A FREE SURPRISE GIFT
★ AND MUCH MORE

TURN THE PAGE AND
DEAL YOURSELF IN

PLAY "LUCKY HEARTS" AND YOU COULD GET...

★ Exciting Silhouette Desire® novels—FREE
★ A folding umbrella—FREE
★ A surprise mystery gift that will delight you—FREE

THEN CONTINUE YOUR LUCKY STREAK WITH A SWEETHEART OF A DEAL

When you return the postcard on the opposite page, we'll send you the books and gifts you qualify for, absolutely free! Then, you'll get 6 new Silhouette Desire novels every month, delivered right to your door months before they're available in stores. If you decide to keep them, you'll pay only $2.24 per book—26¢ less per book than the retail price—and there is no charge for postage and handling. You may return a shipment and cancel at any time.

★ Free Newsletter!

You'll get our free newsletter—an insider's look at our most popular writers and their upcoming novels.

★ Special Extras—Free!

You'll also get additional free gifts from time to time as a token of our appreciation for being a home subscriber.

SILHOUETTE "NO RISK" GUARANTEE

★ You're not required to buy a single book—ever!
★ As a subscriber, you must be completely satisfied or you may return a shipment of books and cancel any time.
★ The free books and gifts you receive from this LUCKY HEARTS offer remain yours to keep—in any case.

If offer card is missing, write to:
Silhouette Book Club, 901 Fuhrmann Blvd., P.O. Box 9013, Buffalo, NY 14240-9013

BUSINESS REPLY CARD

First Class   Permit No. 717   Buffalo, NY

Postage will be paid by addressee

Silhouette Book Club
901 Fuhrmann Blvd.
P.O. Box 9013
Buffalo, NY 14240-9963

NO POSTAGE
NECESSARY
IF MAILED
IN THE
UNITED STATES

Then it was her turn to torture him. She showed no mercy. She devoted special attention to that magnificent spear of flesh and muscle that rose so aggressively between their bodies, caressing him until his teeth were clenched and his breathing impossibly harsh. When he could endure no more, he pushed her hands away, thrust her squealing under the water to wash the soapsuds from her shining skin, and all but dragged her out of the bathtub. He dried her quickly with a bath sheet, lifted her into his arms, and carried her to bed.

"I hope you're not expecting forty-five minutes of sophisticated gymnastics," he said as he followed her down. He settled on top of her, his long, lanky body crushing her into the sheets. Dany automatically parted her legs for him, thrilling to the feeling of him against her downy thatch of curls. "You make me feel about seventeen again, and just as quick on the trigger."

"I don't need forty-five minutes, Max. Two or three ought to do the trick."

Struggling for the last vestiges of his self-control, Max lifted his head. His lover's skin was a lovely rosy ivory, almost translucent, and her full lips were crimson. Her clean, damp hair curved in errant ribbons around her heart-shaped face, and there was the sweetest dimple in the hollow of her throat where her lifeblood beat. Her blue eyes opened as he stared at her, and the corners of that incredibly sexy mouth lifted in the adorable smile that had already stolen what remnants he had of a heart. It was a welcoming smile, a trusting smile. It tempered his lust for just a second, reminding him of all the things she didn't know about him, all the things she was recklessly taking on faith.

"Come to me," she urged him. "It's okay. Now, Max."

Still he hesitated. Not too fast, he was yelling at himself, and not too rough. She was smaller, lighter, and infinitely more delicate than he. Naturally sensual though she was, she might not be prepared for the onslaught he was about to unleash. He didn't want to hurt or frighten her. Yet he wanted her to understand that he considered her irrevocably his.

He shut his eyes. Control. Give her time to get used to you. Give her time to adjust.

But his good resolutions were blasted when she slid her hand between their bodies and caressed him. He jolted as if lightning struck, and a moment later he was driving hard into that warm, welcoming nest. His entire body shivered with the pleasure of being buried deep within the hot silk of her flesh. Dany shivered too, then moaned and clasped her arms around him. Her hips surged up to meet his, and those lovely, long, sexy legs were gripping him tightly now.

Max found her mouth with his. He thrust his tongue in wild syncopation with the driving rhythm of his hips. Dany met him thrust for thrust, giving a series of breathless little cries that turned his bones to water. She was sweet. So tempting, so delicious. That copper hair, running riot on the pillow. Those jutting nipples that responded so exquisitely when he favored them with the slightest, finger-brushing touch.

"Yes, yes," she whispered as his lips slid to the hollow of her throat. The thunder of her heartbeat made him dizzy. He soothed her with his tongue, then nipped her on the pulsepoint, careful not to hurt.

Dany surged beneath him and cried out. Almost immediately he felt her entire body stiffen with her climax. Her nails bit into his shoulders, unconsciously cruel as she reveled in her pleasure. Max smiled. He kissed her throat, her breasts, her mouth, her throat again, rough kisses now, knowing she was beyond pain. Then he levered himself up on his forearms so he could see her slender body writhing beneath him as he continued frantically.

"Dany, Dany," he muttered as he felt his pleasure build and build and finally burst with incredible, shattering force. He collapsed upon her, shuddering, unable to move, barely able to breathe. This isn't sex, he thought groggily. This is ecstasy.

"My lovely girl," he whispered when at last he could speak. "Wow."

She giggled. "Wow?"

"Sounds inarticulate, I know, but I'm at a bit of a loss for words."

"Me too!"

They lay quietly for several minutes, cuddling and gently stroking each other. At length Max said, "I hope we didn't wake Sarah. We've been making a fair amount of noise."

"She sleeps deeply at this time of night. But I'll get up and check her, just as soon as I can move." She rolled over, stretching. "Goodness, Rambler, what did you do to me?" She convulsed in a mammoth yawn. "I don't think I've ever felt so drained."

"I'll check her, Dany. You rest." He kissed her hair and rose from the bed. "I'll peek in and see if she's awake. If so, I won't go in; I'll come get you."

"Okay." It was nice to have a man to check on Sarah. Even when she'd been married to Greg, Dany had always been the one who was expected to rise from a warm bed if her child needed her.

Don't get too accustomed to it, she warned herself. Now that she was satiated, her mind was resuming a more rational cast. It's probably a novelty to him, playing the role of the caring, sensitive male to the lonely single mother. It won't last. And there's no way I'm going to let him draw my daughter close, then push her away like her father did.

Max returned immediately and slid back in beside her. "Sound asleep, the little darling. She's a pretty child. Looks like her mama."

"You're a charmer, Max, you know that?" Another yawn wracked her. "We'd better get some sleep. She wakes up around seven, and you'll have to be gone before then."

"I'm not tired. These are my active hours, remember? I stay up all night." His palms ghosted over her breasts, her belly, her thighs. "We didn't come to bed to sleep, did we, sweetheart? Surely not. I can think of so many better things to do."

"Sure, Max," she said, mischief gleaming in her eyes. "It's too soon. You're all talk."

"Ha!" He tried to grab her as she rolled away, making silly faces at him through the wild curtain of her hair. "So the lady's turning into a tease, is she?"

"Umm-hmm. I'm going to pay you back for all your devilish vampire jokes. Scaring me, dragging me around underground, making me tremble for my throat. Now that I know you're human, I'm going to get even with you, Rambler."

"Yeah?" He cornered her against the headboard. When she playfully struck out at him, nails bared, he clamped her wrists together and rendered her helpless. "What makes you so sure I'm human?"

"Vampires can't do what you just did!"

"You'd be surprised. Vampires can do just about anything, darling, except get a suntan."

She twisted her hands free and ran her palms over his muscled chest. "This is warm, living, human flesh, Max."

He flopped down on his back. "Don't be too sure. Could be an illusion. Vampires are very clever at making people see and feel whatever they want them to. If I were you, I'd conduct a closer examination, just to be on the safe side."

Dany obligingly knelt over him, letting her hair brush his naked skin. She was becoming aroused, she realized. That ache in the pit of her stomach was building all over again.

"You *are* very pale-skinned, I must admit. Not a trace of last summer's suntan. Now if I were superstitious—"

"Which you are."

"—I might be alarmed by that." She kissed his collarbone and the hollow of his throat. "On the other hand, sunbathing is out these days. Everybody's paranoid about skin cancer." She kissed his left nipple, then his right. "So pale skin doesn't prove a thing, does it?" She slid lower in the bed and caressed his hard belly and below. He, too, was aroused, she noted with delight.

"Now, as to the intimate parts of your body, the vampire novels aren't clear on that, unfortunately. What exactly are creatures of the night capable of? They're supposedly dead, so you wouldn't expect them to be able to simulate life in all its forms, would you?"

She kissed him gently. Max arched his back and sighed.

"You taste human. You feel human." Her delicate fingers tormented him. "My goodness, look at that. If all vampires are like you, I'm not surprised they're so legendary."

"Enough," he gasped. He rolled over and jerked her down beside him. Dany went willingly. He was a little rough with her, but she was too awash in desire to care. His eyes were wild and his body a-tremble, but she felt no fear, for the fever was in her, too.

And it escalated. Dany moaned, unaccustomed to this degree of passion. She'd read about obsession and yearning and the kind of white-hot desire that gives no peace, but she'd never really believed they existed. Now, though, her body was burning and her mind was once again a dizzy kaleidoscope of erotic images. She pulled him on top of her. She had to have him inside her again, quickly. She would die if he didn't take her, now, now.

She could hear herself whimpering, pleading with him to join his body to hers. "Shh, love, shh," he whispered. He parted her thighs with his knee. Rough skin, strong muscles, that hard invasive maleness. She fretted for a moment as they were both too clumsy to get it right. He chuckled. "Hold still, love. If you keep writhing around, I can't find you. There. Feel me. There."

His flesh pierced hers. Pleasure, pleasure, great silken clouds of pleasure. Almost instantly, she shattered. She howled her knife-sharp release and exulted in the sound of his hoarse answering cries.

Afterward she was barely conscious. Her soul seemed to float above the bed. "Close your eyes, my love," she heard him whisper. He curled his long limbs around her and stroked her hair rhythmically. "Sleep."

Pressed to his heart, Dany slept as if drugged. Toward morning, she dreamed strange dreams and woke, troubled, unaccountably afraid. Remembering all that had happened between them, she reached out for Max, seeking the comfort of his body, the security of his arms. She felt a warmth in the tangled sheets, but it was only the sunshine streaming in through the open curtains, bathing her body in light. She pushed up on one elbow.

The new day had dawned, and Max Rambler was gone.

Eight

At work, Dany's mind kept wandering back over the sensual events of the night, a pastime that made it exceedingly difficult for her to concentrate. Max was a wonderful lover: aggressive yet tender, masterful yet considerate, insistent yet kind. And that dry humor of his tickled her enormously, even when the laugh was at her own expense.

There was something larger than life about him, something that showed up in the strange, mystical sense of communication that flowed between them when they were making love. The lush images she saw in her head—images that didn't seem to be coming from her own mind. In some ways, it was as if she had a kind of telepathic communion with him during those moments of intense desire, and this was something she'd never experienced before.

Don't get hooked on him, she warned herself. He hadn't been around in the morning, and she didn't know when, or even if, she'd see him again. It might be a good thing if she didn't. Sarah had come into her bedroom around seven-thirty saying, "I dreamed of Max last night, Mommy. I dreamed he was here with us, and that he was going to stay. Are you going to fall in love with Max and marry him, Mom? I hope so. I like him."

Gently, Dany had explained to Sarah that one didn't fall in love and get married quite that easily. "But he's in love with you," Sarah insisted. "I saw the way he was staring at you—his eyes were big and mushy! I know what that means. It means he wants to marry you."

It means he wants to take me to bed, Dany thought with a sigh. How did one explain that to a six-year-old? She did her best to adjust the girl's hopes, and was sorry to see the anticipation leave her daughter's eyes. Sarah had always picked up quickly on unspoken emotions, and she seemed to sense that there was more to the story of Max than her mother was confessing. When Dany had finished telling her that Max had his own life to lead, the child slipped her hand in her mother's and said, "Never mind, Mom. We don't need a man anyway. We have a nice family, just the two of us, don't we?"

"Yes, we do, love. There are all kinds of families, and ours is a fine one."

"I love you, Mom."

"I love you, too, baby."

"Dany?" Cass's voice startled her out of her reverie, jerking her back to her office in the administration building.

"Yes?"

"Thought you'd want to know that I've been asking around about who's into playing Hunt the Night City. Contrary to what David Ellis told you, there can't be too many people involved in this business. I've really got my ear to the ground in this place, and I'm convinced that whatever we have here, it's not a large-scale problem."

"That's something, at least."

"I've heard about some kids who play the board game, and a few who act out the various scenarios in their dorms. But nobody's breathed a word about the tunnels. As far as I can tell, most students have no idea the tunnels exist."

"I was down in them last night, Cass." She had already given him a quick account of her tour through St. Crispin's underworld. "*Somebody's* been using them to play the game. We heard voices, and we found props and scenery. It's possible some of the tunnel adventurers might be members of the drama club."

"Hmm. I'll check it out."

"Anything else to report?"

"Well, I've also been asking about David Ellis. He's something of an enigma. No one knows him very well."

"He's only been at St. Crispin's for a few months. He was a new student last semester."

"He doesn't have a roommate—he lives in a single in the quadrangle. Neither does he appear to have any close friends, with the exception of one student, a girl." Cass paused dramatically. "Guess who."

"I've no idea."

"Jennifer Stokes, your baby-sitter. The scuttlebutt is that she and David are involved with each other."

"As in dating?"

"As in forbidden sexual activity," Cass said with obvious relish. "There's a lot of that on campus, as if you didn't know."

Dany reached up to loosen the clip that held her hair. She'd bound it up too tightly, and her scalp was aching. She remembered the nervousness Jennifer had exhibited when she'd questioned her about David. She'd pretended not to know him very well, yet she'd been concerned that he might be in some kind of trouble.

Dany breathed a long-suffering sigh. "She lied to me, then. I wonder why."

"Probably because Mrs. Kenworthy's edicts still hang heavy over them all. There's a certain paranoia on campus about being caught in a compromising situation with a member of the opposite sex."

"I can see I'm going to have to move a little faster to normalize things around here," Dany said.

"Here's one other detail that might interest you. David's chemistry lab partner told me that David was wrapped up in what he termed a personal quest."

"What sort of personal quest?"

"He wasn't sure, but he thought it had something to do with David's mother."

"What about his mother?"

"Sorry. That's all I know."

She pulled out David's files for another look. There wasn't much information about his mother, just her name—Olivia Ellis—and the fact that she was a divorced interior designer. She looked at the photograph of the boy submitted with his original application to St. Crispin's. His hair was shorter, but otherwise he looked the same. Still, there was something about the picture that disturbed her somehow. She felt a niggling at the back of her mind as she looked into his face, but she couldn't figure out what was causing it. Impatiently, she pushed the folder aside.

"Did you locate Max Rambler's files?"

"Now there's another enigma," said Cass. "I searched the archives this morning and found the files for the years Rambler was here, and I even found a class list with his name upon it. But there was no folder under *R* for Rambler. His records have been removed."

Dany picked up a pencil from her desk and played it back and forth over her rose-tinted fingernails. Max's nails were long and finely kept, unusual in a man. *Vampires have long elegant nails, which gleam as if highly polished.*

Cass gave a sinister laugh. "So you went down into the earth with him last night, huh? Has he turned you into a vampire yet?"

Dany quelled him with a look.

It was later that afternoon that she noticed the mark.

On her way to a meeting with one of the trustees, Dany stopped in the ladies' room to brush her hair and adjust her makeup. While straightening the scarf around her neck, she saw what she first thought to be a shadow or a trick of light. There was an unfamiliar spot on her throat. It was faint, but visible. She moved closer to the mirror to get a better look. It wasn't a bruise—not really—just a distinct darkening of the skin.

She fixed her eyes on the spot, feeling the rush of adrenaline in her blood. It certainly wasn't as dramatic in appearance as the bruise David had shown her. There was no pain when she gingerly fingered it, but when she dabbed a little hot water on the area, hoping it was a stray bit of makeup that would wash off, the mark remained.

Now, don't start, Dany, she ordered herself even as a bizarre scenario suggested itself to her. Suppose, during the night when she'd been deeply asleep, drugged by his loving, Max had silently put his teeth to her throat and driven them in...

"Stop it," she said aloud. She whipped away from the mirror, furious with the suspicions that were crowding her brain. "He kissed you, that's all. He was very passionate about it. If you *still* believe he's a vampire after last night, you really need your head examined. Stop being such an unmitigated jerk."

She knotted her scarf, hiding the spot. No more Stephen King for you, Mistress Faint-of-Heart.

After her meeting, Dany picked up the telephone and dialed Max's number. She wasn't sure exactly what she was going to say when he answered...if he answered. "I'm dead to the world during the daytime," he had told her, but he'd meant it metaphorically, hadn't he?

There was no reply. She tried again several times during the afternoon, but Max never picked up the phone.

Her own phone was ringing that evening when Dany got home. She and Sarah had gone out for supper, then on to the grocery store to pick up a few things. It was nearly eight o'clock, past Sarah's bedtime.

"Where have you been?" Max's voice demanded when she answered. "I've been trying you for hours."

For how many hours exactly, she wondered. Since sunset? "I had some errands to do. Can I call you back? I've got to put Sarah to bed."

"How long until she's asleep?" her demon lover asked. "I'd like to come over."

"It's late, Max, and I'm a little tired."

Silence for a moment. Then he said, "I thought after last night you'd understand that I want to be with you. Every night, Dany."

"I don't recall agreeing to that," she said testily. "We certainly didn't discuss it. You vanished without a word this morning."

"My dear, you were deeply asleep. I didn't want to wake you."

"I tried to call you several times this afternoon, Max. Why didn't you answer the phone?"

"I've got a project I'm working pretty hard on. I was downstairs in the basement lab; I guess I didn't hear the phone."

A likely story. "Max." From the chair where she'd sat to take the call, Dany could see her reflection in the mirror that was hanging over the marble-topped table. She pushed her scarf aside and touched one finger to the rosy mark on her neck. Since she'd last looked it seemed to have darkened slightly.

"What, love? What's the matter? You sound as if you're worried about something."

She frowned. He sounded so normal, so sweet. What was she supposed to say to him—"I have this mark on my throat, and I was wondering if you'd been sucking my blood in the middle of the night"? Somehow she didn't think he would find the accusation amusing. A joke was one thing, but this would be carrying her suspicions ludicrously far.

"I'm still worried about the kids and the tunnels and the game, I suppose," she hedged. "Also, I wish you hadn't left so abruptly last night. I didn't like waking up in the morning alone."

"I'm sorry. I was afraid Sarah was going to bounce in on us. I thought you didn't want me there in the morning."

It would prove you're not a vampire, at least. "I know. You're right, of course. Don't pay any attention to me. It's been a long day."

His voice was tender. "Poor baby. I can help you relax. May I come down?"

"No, Max. Not tonight."

She heard him sigh. "Tomorrow night? Would you prefer to come here? We'll have more privacy. Do you think you could get a baby-sitter?"

She felt herself weaken. "For a couple of hours, perhaps. Not for the entire night."

"A couple of hours is better than nothing," he said resignedly. "Do you want me to lay in something for supper? I'm afraid I'm pretty hopeless when it comes to cooking."

It would have been nice to see him eat like a normal human being, but he sounded so dismayed at the idea of having to provide a meal for her that she took pity on him. "No, don't bother. I'll feed Sarah, get her ready for bed and then come." She had a brainstorm. "Tell you what, I'll bring over something for dessert."

"Dessert, huh?" His voice was so sexy it practically burned up the telephone line. "I love dessert." He paused. "But I wouldn't want to put you to any trouble."

"No trouble, Max. No trouble at all."

"See you tomorrow, then."

"Good night, Max."

"Dany?"

"Yes?" Her mind was flooded with erotic images. Once again she had the eerie feeling that they were coming telepathically from him.

"Think of me," he said huskily, and hung up.

Dany thought she detected the tiniest trace of dismay in her lover's expression when she did indeed show up at his Gothic mansion the following evening with a pint of chocolate-chunk pecan ice cream. Nevertheless, he proved to be a courteous host. Within ten minutes they were seated at a long cherrywood table in the elegant, if slightly dusty, dining room, eating the rich dessert from beautiful sterling-silver bowls.

Dany, at least, was eating hers. Max seemed to be eating his—the spoon was going in and out of his mouth, anyway—but she couldn't be absolutely sure. The room was lighted only by candles, and the table was so huge that their chairs were several feet away from each other.

There was something about the atmosphere of the place that made Dany uneasy. "Why do you live in a house like this?" she asked him. "When I come here I feel as if I've entered another century."

"I like it."

"But Max, it's so archaic and formal. It doesn't really feel lived-in, if you know what I mean. When are you going to get the lights fixed?"

"Maybe never. The candlelight's romantic, don't you think?"

"Did you move in recently?" she asked, anxious to find some explanation for the condition of the place.

He looked at her for a long moment in silence, then said, "I work hard, Dany. I don't have time to renovate my house, nor am I particularly interested in doing so. It suits me fine the way it is. It's a pleasant change."

"From what?" she asked, mystified.

"From the environment in which I work."

"What exactly do you mean? I thought you worked here at home."

"I do, but my basement lab is considerably more modern than the rest of this place."

"Will you take me down there? I'd like to see where you work."

"Sorry. The lab's off limits."

She blinked, surprised not only by his words but also by the uncompromising manner of his speech. "What do you mean? Why?"

"I'm working on the frontiers of the high-tech industry, that's why. I'm doing stuff nobody else has done, and until I'm ready to go public with it, it has to be kept securely under wraps."

"What do you think I am, a computer-industry spy?"

"Of course not. But you wouldn't like my lab, Dany." There was something very stark about his tone of voice, something closed and cold about his expression. "Nor do you really want to know anything about my work. Let's talk about something else, okay? Any new leads on the identity of the Ancient One?"

He didn't like to talk about himself. Despite their new intimacy, that, it seemed, wasn't going to change.

Dany felt a chord of sorrow deep inside her. He has such a solitary look. Why did he insist on cutting her off; why cut himself off and live alone, work alone on the very fringes of society? Was he hiding something? Why would a man who was so tender and considerate in bed deny himself all other forms of human contact?

These were questions she wanted to ask him, but not now, not yet. Working with teenagers had taught her that you couldn't force a confidence.

"No new leads," she said.

"How about faculty members?"

"Well, if we're going to start suspecting faculty members, I can think of one or two likely candidates. There's a guy in the English department who writes extremely bizarre poetry and is known for his misanthropic nature. He even looks like a vampire."

"How does a vampire look?"

"Oh, I don't know. Graceful, quick-moving, with pale skin and luminous, hypnotic eyes."

Max half smiled at her, his luminous, hypnotic eyes holding hers captive. She really hadn't intended to describe him so pointedly.

"I should think a vampire would look exactly as he had looked when he was human," he said. "Before some other vampire took him and initiated him into the fraternity of the undead. He could be dark-skinned or light, blond or redhead, graceful and hypnotic and all those other romantic things, or just plain ordinary."

"We're not talking about real vampires, Max."

"But what if we are? What if it's all even more sinister than we think? What if a real vampire is using Hunt the Night City as a cloak, an excuse to live according to his own nature?"

"Get serious," she said weakly.

"If vampires existed, it would be a perfect cover, you'll have to admit."

"Well, they don't," she said, even as her fingers nervously touched the high collar that hid the mark on her throat.

To Dany's relief, he dropped this line of discussion and went on to tell her that he'd spent the previous night down in the tunnels again. "I didn't see or hear anybody else down there last night, but I did find a couple of other chambers that had been set up to resemble various scenes in the game. I guess they don't play every single night."

This fit in with what Cass had told her. "Maybe there's only one group. Just David and a few of his friends from the drama club. God, I hope so."

"Have you pried anything else out of David, by the way?"

She mentioned what she'd heard from Cass about David's personal quest. "His mother, huh?" said Max. "Who is she, do you know?"

"Her name is Olivia Ellis. Apparently she's divorced from David's father. She and David used to live on the West Coast, but now she works in Boston and sends him to school here."

She stopped. Max had made a sharp movement. Dany could see from the expression on his face that something she'd said had shocked him. "What's the matter? Do you know her?"

Max put his spoon down carefully on the table beside his dish. She could see that his knuckles were white. "I knew an Olivia, once. But her last name wasn't Ellis."

Dany waited. She sensed there was something more. But several seconds went by and Max did not speak. She leaned toward him. "What's the matter?"

For an instant she thought he was going to answer her. Then something tightened around his mouth, and she knew he was not. *Oh Max, why don't you trust me? Is it so hard for you to trust?*

"I'd like to have a talk with David," was all he said. "Do you suppose that can be arranged?"

"I imagine so."

"There might not be an Ancient One, you realize, Dany. Maybe the boy made up the story of my alleged attack as a way of calling your attention to me."

"But why?"

"I'm not sure why, but you can bet I'm going to find out. Now enough of this." He looked at his watch, then pushed back his mammoth chair and stood. He moved to the back of her chair and laid his hands on her shoulders. "Time's a-wasting. Come kiss me, Headmistress. I've gazed at you from afar for long enough this evening."

Dany found the change in subject and mood a little difficult to cope with. Even so, she went without reluctance into his arms. But as he bent her head back and fiercely took her mouth, some impulse made her open one eye and look beyond him. Joe the cat had jumped up on the arm of Max's vacated chair. He was avidly licking the untouched ice cream in his master's silver bowl.

Dany stayed another hour. Max took her upstairs to a huge, darkened bedroom, laid her down on an oaken bed-stead that looked to be of the same vintage as the dining room set and stripped her of her clothes. He proceeded to make exquisite love to her, making her feel wanton and obsessed. Without mercy, he teased her. By the time he finally joined his body to hers, she was out of her head; she'd have bartered her soul to the devil if that had been the payment for having him inside her.

Yet, in spite of her sensual delirium, Dany's nervousness never entirely dissipated. Passionate though she felt, every time his mouth wandered in the direction of her throat, which happened all too frequently, she tensed and opened her eyes. She expected him to notice and comment upon her odd behavior, but he didn't. In fact, he seemed just a touch preoccupied himself.

Later, curled in his arms, listening to the slow rhythms of his breathing, Dany stretched and whispered, "Max, I've got to go."

"Stay a little longer. You feel so good beside me. Relax, my love, and rest from your heroic exertions."

That was the trouble—her exertions had worn her out, but she was afraid to fall asleep, even for a few minutes. She didn't want to wake up later to find a new mark on her throat. Oh, she knew she was being silly, but there was something about this spooky house and this dark, cavernous bedroom that activated all her most absurd superstitions. By the weak light of the flashlight he'd used when he'd brought her upstairs, she'd noted that there were no personal things in the room, no clothes or shoes or male toiletries lying around. No clock beside the bed, no lamp, no radio, no books for bedtime reading. This wasn't his bedroom, it couldn't be. Why hadn't he taken her to his bedroom? And why had he only pretended to eat his ice cream?

Vampires can do anything, except get a suntan. She sat up, overcome by a strong urge to flee from this creepy place. "I have to get home to Sarah."

"I know. I'll let you go soon." He pulled her back down and pressed her flat, entwining his long limbs with hers. "But not yet."

She struggled, alarmed by this playful demonstration of his superior strength. Max liked her and didn't want to hurt her, she was certain of that. But everyone knew that the nicest, most affectionate vampire could turn ugly when seized with an overpowering thirst for blood.

"Max?"

"What?"

One comment, she'd allow herself one comment. She'd say it, and see how he reacted. "Do you think I'll ever see you by the light of day?"

He smiled that wicked, mischievous little-boy smile, the one that deepened his laugh lines and melted her right down to her bones. "You wouldn't want to see me turn to ash before your very eyes, would you?"

He was joking. Of course he was joking. She was determined to joke right back: "Gee, Rambler, no. At least, not as long as you continue to be so awesome in bed."

The grin widened. "Awesome? You sound like one of those teenagers you hang around with." He slid a hand over her flesh, lightly grazing her breast, her belly, her thigh. She felt an undeniable quickening within her. There *was* something supernatural about him. Only a moment before she would have said she was thoroughly sated.

Max found her mouth with his, and she felt the same quickening within him. "Totally awesome," she whispered as his ready body covered hers again.

Max Rambler watched his lover as she drove away from his house into the night. Once again his big cat was in his arms. "You're all I have to cuddle to, Joe, now that my lady is gone."

But Joe was not in the mood to be cuddled this time. He fought, even showing his claws, and his master let him down. "What's the matter? Jealous? You get plenty of attention, you old fleabag of a cat. Anyway, what are you complaining about? You ate a whole damn dish of ice cream, didn't you? When was the last time you got a treat like that?"

Max sighed. It was a crystal night, with stars so bright they seemed to tear holes of jagged light through the black fabric of the sky. He loved this kind of night. He couldn't think of many things he'd rather do than be out in it, stalking through the darkness, breathing the cold, crisp air. He'd always loved the night. Even as a kid at St. Crispin's, back in the days of his youth and innocence, it had not been until after the sun went down that he had really come alive. Darkness had been a friend to him. It had cloaked and protected him, given him permission, granted him space. Midnight Rambler, one of his few friends had called him, even then. Midnight Rambler he was and forever would be.

He thought of Dany's bright, coppery hair and the way it flamed like the rising sun. And of her eyes, the vibrant blue of a clear summer day. "You're all wrong for her," he muttered. He thought of the questions she'd asked, about his work, about his life. Questions he hadn't dared to answer.

"She knows nothing about you, which is the only reason she puts up with you. She knows nothing, and fool that you are, you're doing your best to keep it that way. But how long do you suppose that will last? Sooner or later she'll hear the gossip, the old rumors that haven't died. How long do you think you can keep your finger in the dike before the whole thing blows up around you?

Max slammed the door and shut out the night. He went into his study and opened his desk, removing the file he had stolen from the St. Crispin's archives. His own file, full of the details that he didn't want Dany to learn. It had come to him fairly early on that he couldn't allow her to get a look at the file. The rest would be rumor, but in his file were the facts.

It had been easy to steal it. He'd done it late the other night, after slipping from her bed. The tunnels under the school were useful for other things besides playing Hunt the

Night City, and it apparently hadn't occurred to Dany yet that since the house she lived in was an official school residence, it, too, was linked by the tunnels to the other buildings on campus. It had been no problem to gain access to the administration building archives from the tunnel that opened into her basement.

"At least she won't ever be able to shut me out, even if she does find out the truth," he said out loud. "Even if she locks her doors, I can get into her house, into her bed. I can force her to listen while I attempt to explain. I'll have a chance, at least, no matter what happens."

It was a small consolation. Some things were too dark to explain.

Nine

When Max called the following night, Dany said in a rush, "Oh, Max, Sarah's sick and I can't reach her regular pediatrician. I hate it when she's sick. It's the only time I miss that blasted Greg, not that he was ever very good with a sick child."

"What's wrong with her?"

"High fever and a sore throat. It's probably strep, which always scares me because of the possible complications. She needs a throat culture. I was just about to drive her to a clinic in North Conway to get it done."

"North Conway's thirty miles away, and it's snowing."

"I know. That's what I hate about these small towns! In San Diego there was always a clinic nearby if I couldn't reach our family doctor. I lived too long in California, I guess."

"Sit tight, love, and wait for me. I'll drive you and Sarah to North Conway."

"Oh no, I didn't mean to impose on you. It's a long ride and besides, if it's strep she's contagious."

"I never get sick, but even if I did, that wouldn't stop me. It's a bad night, and you need a driver who's used to the roads. I'll be down in about ten minutes, okay? Bundle Sarah up and be ready for me."

It didn't occur to Dany to resent his masculine take-charge attitude. Sarah's fever was almost one hundred and four, and she was thankful for his offer of help.

They made the trip in Max's black Porsche, she and Sarah safely ensconced in the passenger seat while Max drove confidently through snow and sleet along the mountainous roads. The doctor in North Conway confirmed that the infection looked enough like strep to start Sarah on an antibiotic while they were waiting for the results of the throat culture. Max found an all-night pharmacy and bought the medication while Dany held Sarah and comforted her. The child's fever had made her unusually wan and silent. But when Max returned with her medicine, a chewable form of penicillin, Sarah managed a smile.

"I'll bet it tastes awful," she said.

"The pharmacist assured me it tastes just like bubble gum." He opened the plastic bottle and presented one of the pink tablets to Sarah, who obediently popped it into her mouth.

"It does taste like bubble gum. Thank you, Max. My mommy's medicines always taste yucky."

"Where in heaven's name did you get bubble-gum-flavored penicillin?" asked Dany a little later when Sarah fell asleep in her arms.

"It's really cherry-flavored, I think."

"Then it's the same stuff I give her. The stuff she thinks is yucky."

He winked at her. "One of my powers—changing the taste, smell, feel or appearance of something such as to deceive my victims."

Dany laughed. "I should have known you couldn't let the evening pass without at least one vampire crack."

"Must keep up my sinister image."

"Max, thank you," she said later as they stood on the threshold of Sarah's bedroom, watching the feverish girl sleep. "I'm by no means a helpless or dependent woman, but I can't deny it felt good to have a man around tonight. I hate it when she's sick, Max. I get so scared. Sometimes I think I must have lost a beloved child in a former life to some awful childhood disease."

"You believe in former lives?"

"I think so. The idea makes a lot of sense to me."

"I do, too. I've known you before, Dany. We've been lovers many times."

How wonderful if that were true. Perhaps that was why she felt so close to him, even though there was so much she didn't know about him. Perhaps that was why she trusted him, unconventional though he was.

Max kissed her mouth, a comradely kiss, not an erotic one. "Get some sleep, sweetheart. You look tired. I'm wide-awake, as always at this time of night. I'll sit up and keep an eye on her in case her fever spikes again."

"You don't have to—"

"I want to. Let me, please."

She knew she ought to protest that things were moving too fast between them, to remind him again that his plunging into a fatherly role would hurt Sarah if things didn't work out. Especially since—in this life at least—she'd known him for less than a week. But she was tired, and it felt so good to have him nearby.

"Don't look so worried, Dany. Have a little faith in me."
He took her arm and walked her across the hall to her own
bedroom. "Now get in there and rest."

A less caring man might have accompanied her to bed,
she thought sleepily as she curled up under the blankets. She
wouldn't have refused his lovemaking, exhausted though she
was. Their affair was still so new that her desire for him was
almost constant, and she knew it was the same for him.
During their brief embrace she'd felt the hard demand of his
body, the need he had to fall into bed beside her and seek
relief. Generously, he was controlling that desire so she
could rest.

She liked him. He was sensitive and considerate, so good
with her daughter, so pleasant to have around.

You're falling for him, Dany. You're falling hard.

She was asleep almost instantly, dreaming of other times
and other places, with Max Rambler always there at her
side.

If she'd had doubts before, Dany learned within the next
few nights that Max had been absolutely serious when he'd
referred to his lovemaking as a claiming. He no longer
bothered to call and make a formal date with her. He simply appeared, without fail, every evening after sunset—and
after dinner, too, she noted with some dismay—settling into
her life with proprietary ease.

Despite her misgivings, he became best pals with Sarah,
taking genuine delight in getting down on the floor with her
and playing one game after another. He told her stories and
helped in her fledgling attempts to read the first-grade
primers. He listened gravely while she recounted her day at
school, always treating her with an affable respect that Dany
had found to be rare in adults who were not parents. He
didn't hesitate to speak sternly to her if Sarah misbehaved,
which Sarah did not seem to resent in the least. Indeed, be-

fore the week was out, it was evident that the little girl adored him.

She wasn't the only one. Dany's feelings grew stronger every day. The sexual infatuation continued, but sex was only one channel for the intuitive communication that had sprung up between them. She felt free and whole with him; she could truly be herself. He made her laugh. He touched her heart.

Even so, in many ways he remained a mystery. He turned aside all questions about his past, sometimes with a harshness that upset her. He rarely spoke about his work. He didn't eat, or at least not in her presence. He entered her home with such silence and stealth that his appearance would often make Dany jump with surprise.

"How did you get in?" she asked him several times. "All the doors are locked."

He laughed and put on a fake Transylvanian accent. "How foolish you are, my lovely lady, to think a lock vill keep me out."

Over the course of the next few nights, Max made several more forays into the tunnels. Although he found nobody playing the game, he reported afterward to Dany that he had an uncanny feeling that someone was down there, watching him. "Someone who knows those tunnels even better than I do. Someone agile and quick on his feet. Someone whose night vision is as good as mine."

"Another vampire, I suppose?"

"Another master vampire, my dear. I'm no slouch at this, you know."

"You mean there's someone around here who's better at playing Hunt the Night City than you are? The Ancient One, perhaps?"

"I doubt he's particularly ancient. I'd put his age at about sixteen."

"You think it's David, don't you?"

"He leaves messages down there. Catch-me-if-you-can sort of thing. The kid is taunting me, Dany. I want to know why."

"I asked him if he would agree to meet you and have a talk. 'No way,' he said. He looked horrified at the prospect."

"He can't avoid me forever," Max said in an ominous tone.

"Please don't seek him out yourself. For whatever absurd reason, he's frightened of you."

"Sounds to me as if he needs a few sessions with the school shrink."

Dany didn't know what to think. By the end of the week the mystery was no closer to being solved. But at least none of the other students had been attacked by someone masquerading as the Ancient One. When David had first come to her with his story, she'd been afraid of an epidemic, but it hadn't developed. "It seems that I'm the only one with marks on my throat these days," she said to herself wryly. She had taken to wearing high-necked sweaters to disguise the faint but regularly appearing signs of Max Rambler's passion.

Toward the end of the month, Dany spent a hectic Friday in a conference with three sets of wealthy parents who were considering St. Crispin's for their children. She then attended a long, boring meeting in the humanities building, so it was midafternoon before she got back to her office. She found a very pale Jennifer Stokes waiting there for her.

"She's been here for over an hour," Cass explained. "I tried to find out what was wrong, but she wouldn't speak to anybody except you."

"Come into my office, Jen. We can talk privately there."

As the teenager took a seat in front of Dany's desk, Dany noticed that her hands were clasped so tightly together her knuckles were white. "What on earth is the matter?"

"I'm not supposed to be here," the girl began. "I shouldn't be talking to you, but I didn't know who else to turn to."

"I'm glad you came to me," Dany said gently. "You can trust me to help you, Jennifer. Whatever the trouble is, we'll deal with it together."

Jennifer took a deep breath. "It's about David. I...I sort of misled you about us."

"You're dating him, aren't you?"

The girl looked astonished. "You knew?"

Dany nodded. When Jennifer flushed, she added, "It's all right. Unlike my predecessor, I don't believe in interfering with the personal lives of my students. Anyway, that's not the reason you're here, I take it. You haven't come to me about problems with your love life."

Jennifer shook her head. "No. It's something else." She hesitated for a moment, then went on, "I'm worried about him, Ms. Holland. He's into this vampire game, and I'm scared. He's obsessed with it."

Dany nodded. She was beginning to think so, too.

"He's particularly obsessed with Max Rambler. I don't know why, Ms. Holland. It's weird. I don't know if he really thinks the guy is a vampire or what, but I'm sure he thinks Mr. Rambler is evil."

"Evil?" The word sounded ridiculous, especially when applied to Max.

"I didn't believe him at first. But now—" She paused, and her eyes filled up with tears. "Oh, Ms. Holland, now he's disappeared."

Dany stiffened. "David's disappeared?"

"Yes. Nobody's seen him all day. He's not in his dorm; he wasn't in class today. And his bed wasn't slept in last night."

Dany felt the beginnings of a headache thread through her temples. Blast the boy! This was precisely the sort of thing she'd hoped to avoid.

"I've been looking for him all day," the girl went on. "He's not in the library, not in the gym, not in any of the usual places. I'm afraid he went somewhere last night and didn't come back."

"Where do you think he went?"

"To Mr. Rambler's house." Jennifer's eyes were huge now. "David said something about having a rendezvous with the vampire. I thought he was kidding. I thought it was just part of the game. But now I think he meant it. He went to Rambler's house at midnight and he never came back. Please, Ms. Holland, I'm frightened. What if Rambler really is a vampire? What if he attacked David again and this time sucked his neck until he died?"

Dany pushed away from her desk to pace back and forth in the room. "For the last time, vampires don't exist! And as for Max Rambler, he's harmless. He's certainly not evil." Unconsciously, Dany touched her throat, concealed under the soft wool of a turtleneck sweater. Max hadn't spent last night with her. He'd told her he had to work. "He's a kind, charming, considerate man."

"All I know is that David is gone. Look at this. Please." Jennifer opened her pocketbook and took a crumpled piece of paper out. "I found this in David's room a little while ago. It was beside the phone."

Dany unfolded the paper. It was from a small pad, the sort of thing one might keep beside the telephone to write messages on. Scribbled in pencil were the words, "Sharp turnoff at top of Glencrag on left. Signpost at turn. Curving gravel driveway. Big stone house with gargoyles, no number. Black Porsche in garage. Midnight tonight.''

"It sounds as if someone was giving him directions, doesn't it?'' said Jennifer.

Dany swallowed hard. *He's my lover. I wouldn't make love to a man capable of hurting a child, would I? Surely some instinct would warn me. Surely I'd be able to sense the rottenness lurking beneath the facade.* "Have you ever been to Max Rambler's house?'' she asked.

The girl shook her head. "But I've heard it's a big stone house with gargoyles, and I know he drives a black Porsche.''

"Okay. Look, I'll check it out. Go back to your dormitory and stop worrying. If David's with Max, he's safe. Max would never hurt him.'' She crossed to Jennifer and hugged her. "We'll find him, Jen, I promise you that.''

As soon as she left the office, Dany picked up the phone and called Max. As usual—damn him—the number rang and rang without any answer.

Dany dialed campus security. Within ten minutes, Ed Berry, the beefy fifty-year-old head of the campus police, was seated opposite her. "Probably run off to see some girl,'' he said, when he heard Dany's slightly expurgated version of David's disappearance. "It's happened before, you know. Place is too strict, if you ask me.''

"Do any of your men patrol the entrances to the old tunnels that lie underneath the campus?''

"The tunnels? Naw. Those tunnels have been boarded up for years. I assure you, nobody could get into those.''

She raised her eyebrows skeptically.

"We had some trouble with those tunnels years ago, and Mrs. Kenworthy ordered them shut up tight. It's a maze down there, and for some weird reason, the tunnels were a temptation to some of the kids.''

"What sort of trouble?''

The color came up in Ed Berry's cheeks. "Ah, you don't know about that? No, of course you don't. Guess I shouldn't have said anything."

"Tell me."

He was looking none too pleased. "Me and my big mouth. I'm not supposed to tell anybody—Jeez, I never have told anybody. The scandal, about seventeen years ago it must be, was hushed up at the time. I just thought you'd have heard about it, being headmistress and all."

"Look, we've got a missing child here, Ed. And this is only the latest in a series of odd events. Something very strange is going on here at St. Crispin's, and it involves those tunnels. I want to know everything there is to know about them, including any wild tales of scandal."

"But those tunnels are inaccessible, boarded up."

"I was down in them myself a few nights ago." She watched the expression on his face change. "That's right. I nearly got lost down there, too, when my flashlight conked out. I want to hear what happened in the tunnels, Ed. Now, if you please."

Berry sighed. "A girl was abducted one night back in 1970. She was seventeen years old and a senior here. At first we thought she'd run off with some boy, but that wasn't likely, considering who she was."

"Who was she?"

"She'd been raised real strict, you see. A good girl of high moral character, not the type to do anything she wasn't supposed to do. She wasn't one of those fast girls, no, not her."

"Who was she, Ed? I'll keep this confidential, if need be, but I have to know."

He shrugged helplessly. "She was the headmistress's daughter."

"Mrs. Kenworthy's daughter?" This was the last thing she'd expected to hear. Despite the seriousness of the subject, Dany felt an irreverent desire to burst out laughing. She controlled the impulse with some difficulty. The strict headmistress's daughter involved in a scandal? No wonder it had been hushed up. "Go on."

"Her mother, naturally, was beside herself. I mean, everybody immediately jumped to the conclusion that she'd eloped with some male. People were talking, saying Mrs. Kenworthy was a hypocrite who couldn't keep discipline in her own home. She was a proud woman. In some ways, it was almost a relief for her when the ransom note came. It meant the girl hadn't just gone off of her own free will."

"If it were my daughter, I'd rather she'd gone off of her own free will than been stolen away by someone who meant her harm."

"Yeah, me too, but you must remember this happened a while ago. Edith Kenworthy had made her reputation as a disciplinarian during a time when discipline was starting to go out of fashion. The late sixties were not good years for St. Crispin's, as you can probably imagine."

"Who were the kidnappers?"

"Kidnapper," he corrected. "There was only one. He was just a kid himself, one of her classmates. A shy boy who'd been crazy about the Kenworthy girl for months but hadn't known how to go about getting her to notice him. At least, that's the way we figured it later."

Dany's heart had begun to pound. A shy boy. Oh God. The tunnels, seventeen years ago, no records in the file . . .

Berry was continuing, oblivious. "Somehow or other he coaxed her into the tunnels. He got her there, and he refused to let her out. He, uh, made advances to her, and when she refused him he tied her up in one of the underground chambers and raped her, poor girl. At least, that's the tale she told her mother afterward, and there's no reason to doubt it was the truth. As I said, she was a well-brought-up girl."

"What happened to the boy?" Dany asked dully.

"That was the odd thing. You'd have thought Mrs. Kenworthy would have made sure the kid went to prison, but as it turned out, he got lucky. He was never even arraigned. The headmistress was terrified about scandal, you see, and people were even more reluctant to press charges in rape cases than they are now. It's always been hard to get a conviction.

"No, he got off easy," Berry went on. "He was expelled. His parents were wealthy, and no doubt they made some sort of settlement with Mrs. Kenworthy. They left town, taking their son with them, and hushed it up, I guess. Good thing, too. The kid went on to make something of himself, which he might not have been able to do if this sort of scandal had followed him around."

"Who was he?" There was a cold feeling in the pit of Dany's stomach. Please, she said to herself. Not Max, please.

"It's funny," Berry said slowly, "But I remember the kid insisting that he hadn't done it, that he'd never sent the ransom note that tipped us off, that Mrs. Kenworthy had made up the whole thing to protect her daughter's reputation. Quite passionate about it, he was. No one believed him, of course. He even swore to come back and prove it someday. He did come back, too. A couple of years ago. But people seem to have forgotten, if indeed they ever knew he was the perpetrator."

Dany's cold feeling had spread throughout her body. "You're talking about Max Rambler, aren't you?"

Berry nodded. He looked at her curiously. "How did you catch on to that so fast? Have you heard this story before, after all?"

"I know Mr. Rambler slightly," she said noncommittally.

"And he told you something about it? He's done all right for himself, hasn't he?"

"Oh Max," she said under her breath. Her hands were clenched in her lap. No wonder she hadn't been able to find his student files. Somebody—maybe even Max himself—had destroyed them to cover up this entire ugly affair. "Is there any chance the girl may have been lying?" she asked.

Berry shrugged. "She was quite specific in her accusations. She wrote it all out, what he'd done to her, and it was pretty graphic. She wasn't the imaginative type, as far as I could see. And Rambler, although shy and quiet on the surface, struck me as a pretty explosive guy. Was he capable of such a thing? Yeah, I think he was. Is he still? Maybe not. People change. He must be what—thirty-five?—not a wild kid anymore. But he's lucky he got off, if you ask me."

Dany imagined his face, tender and amused, his hands oh-so-gentle as he loved her. He was a patient, considerate lover, as desirous of her pleasure as he was of his own. Max a rapist? Impossible.

But suddenly she remembered him as he had been on the night they'd met, his supple mouth hardened into a tight line, his eyes blazing with fury as he'd deliberately frightened her in retaliation for an accusation he had not wanted to hear. She'd seen no evidence of that mood in him since, but hadn't that moment proved him capable of at least some degree of violence?

"I hadn't realized before that Mrs. Kenworthy had a daughter. Did she leave town too?"

"Yes," Berry confirmed. "Married some guy and went out to the West Coast. Seattle, I believe. Got divorced a year later—too young, I guess. I haven't heard anything about poor little Olivia since."

"Olivia?"

"That was her name."

Dany sat without breathing. She stared at her finger-nails. One of them was chipped. Her hands were shaking slightly. The palms were damp.

"The man she married, do you happen to remember his name?" She remembered the look on Max's face when she'd told him the name of David's mother. "Was it Ellis, by any chance?"

"Could have been. Yeah, that sounds familiar. Ellis. Why? Hey, wait a minute. Isn't Ellis the name of the boy who's missing?"

The kid is taunting me, Max had said. *I want to know why.* Oh God. You raped his mother, Max. That's reason enough, don't you think?

"Drew Ellis, that was her husband's name," said Berry.

"Excuse me." Dany jumped up and sprinted out of her office, crashing into Cass, who was at the door with a yellow note card in his hand. He caught her and steadied her, hardly noticing her agitation because of his own.

"Hey, I was just coming to tell you, Dany. I finally got something on the mysterious Mr. Rambler. No file yet, but listen to this: he was expelled in 1970 for conduct unbefitting a gentleman. Now what do you suppose that means?"

Dany didn't stop to answer.

Ten

—

For once it was still daylight when Dany arrived at the Gothic mansion Max called home. "Good," she said out loud as she mounted the wide stone steps. "Now we'll find out once and for all whether you really spend the day in a coffin."

No one answered her loud knocking. When she put her hand to the doorknob and twisted, she found the door wasn't locked. Creaking, it swung open. "Max? Max! It's Dany! Are you here?"

There was still no answer. She entered anyway. She didn't think he'd gone anywhere, because she'd passed the garage and seen the snub-nosed Porsche inside. Was he sleeping? It was late afternoon, and even if he did sleep during the day, surely he'd be up and about by now.

"Max!" No reply. "David?" she tried. Her voice echoed eerily through the place, which, even by day, was dark and gloomy inside. There was a faint dry smell of age and antiques, but no familiar homey scents, like food or soaps or flowers.

Where was he, dammit? And where was David? Max had wanted to talk to the boy for several days, and finally it seemed that David had agreed. But why last night at midnight? What had happened between them? Had David admitted to being Olivia Kenworthy's son? Had he accused Max of raping his mother?

Oh, Max, I wish you'd told me. I wish I knew what to believe.

She walked through the hall to an archway that lead into the front parlor. She couldn't remember ever having been in this particular room before. She'd only been in the house twice, and on neither occasion had her host taken her for a tour. She flicked a light switch on the wall. Nothing happened. Heavy drapes curtained the windows, and most of the furniture was covered with sheets.

"If I didn't know somebody lived in this place, I'd think it was unoccupied," she said aloud. Talking made her feel better. Every time she entered this mausoleum she felt the hair on the back of her neck rise.

Dany let out a yelp when something furry rubbed against her legs, then realized it was Max's cat, Joe. She gathered him up into her arms and pressed her face against his warm, thick fur. He started purring immediately. "Where's your master, Joe?" she whispered. "Good kitty. He's kind to you, isn't he? You wouldn't be so affectionate if he were not."

A few minutes spent petting the cat helped Dany gather her wits. She put the beast down. "Lead me to Max," she said, following the cat as he made off down a hallway toward the rear of the house. They entered the kitchen, which had never been modernized. There was an archaic gas stove, but no dishwasher or refrigerator. How could he manage without a refrigerator?

She opened a cupboard, then another. The few dishes looked as though they'd never been used. "I can't cook," Max had asserted several times. "I spend a fortune every month at the local McDonald's."

She opened several other cupboards. The only food she found was for the cat.

"This is crazy," she said to Joe. "Nobody could live like this—it's just not possible."

Vampires don't eat or drink.

Stop it, Dany!

The cat rubbed against her legs and looked hopefully at the cupboard that held the cans of cat food. Dany obliged, dishing some out into the plastic plate she found neatly washed beside the sink. Joe attacked the food with obvious pleasure. "It's nice to see *someone* around here eat," said Dany wryly.

"Where's your master?" she asked again when the big cat had finished devouring the food and was daintily licking his paws. Joe gazed up at her intelligently, then turned and trotted off. Once again she followed.

The cat led her through the hall to the front of the house. At the foot of the stairs leading to the second story, he stopped. His tail swished back and forth a couple of times. He looked at her expectantly.

Dany gazed up the wide staircase. It disappeared into shadows. "Why didn't I bring a flashlight?" she wondered aloud. "I wouldn't go down into the tunnels so ill prepared. Oh well. Come on, cat."

Joe gave her a disdainful look and lay down on the hall carpet.

Feeling like the heroine of one of her beloved Gothic novels, she climbed the grand old staircase. At the top was a long corridor running perpendicular to the stairs. Several doors lined the hallway. Doggedly, she opened each of them, calling her lover's name as she went, looking into one beautiful bedroom after another. He had brought her up here a few nights ago, but she wasn't sure to which room he'd carried her. She'd been too drugged by his loving to notice.

The bedrooms were all exquisitely furnished. But she saw no evidence of Max's possessions, nothing to indicate that any of these rooms was where he slept. They were cold and impersonal, lifeless. And they were dusty, as if no living soul had set foot inside for months. Had he really made love to her in one of these passionless chambers? It had been dark that night, and she'd seen so little of her surroundings.

"Last chance, Rambler," she muttered when she reached the final door at the end of the hall. "This one had better be your bedroom, complete with your clothes, your shoes, your razor and your deodorant. Otherwise I'm not letting you near me again until you prove you're human."

She twisted the handle. Nothing happened. "Dammit."

She jiggled the knob. Her palm, damp with sweat, slipped on the smooth metal. She started to call out, then choked back the cry. She had a nasty image—idiotic, of course—but she couldn't get it out of her mind. She envisioned another room, cold like the others, furnished with priceless antiques. The chamber was dominated by an enormous catafalque upon which rested an ornate coffin. She imagined herself opening the lid and looking into his pale, still face. He'd know she was there. He'd know it, but he'd be frozen, unable to rise from his deathly slumber. He'd be helpless for the next few minutes until the sun went down.

She swallowed convulsively. How much time was left before the night? When the red sun slid behind the horizon and the vampire arose, he would be ravenous. He'd be so starved for blood he'd pounce on the first living creature he saw. According to every lurid account she'd ever read on the subject, a vampire's passion for blood was fierce and completely impersonal. He was at his most dangerous when he first awoke; after drinking his nightly ration of blood, a vampire could be remarkably civilized, even friendly.

Like Max.

Dany's thoughts were out of control, ravaged by the full force of her imagination. Thoroughly unnerved, she turned and fled down the hall to the wide oaken staircase.

"Coward!" she reproached herself when she gained the first floor. "Superstitious idiot. You're a grown woman. This is a man you've taken to yourself, body-to-body, soul-to-soul. He's kind, gentle, affectionate and a wonderful lover. And if he's ever committed a crime, it was rape, not blood-drinking."

She found her way to the book-lined study where they'd spoken on the night they'd met. The room was a little warmer than the rest of the house. She sank down onto the sofa.

Olivia had lied, of course. It was the only explanation Dany would accept. Better to say she was kidnapped and sexually assaulted than to admit she'd run away with Max of her own free will.

Joe appeared to rub against her legs again. "You're a big help," she said to him. "Why did you let me go upstairs alone?"

Joe purred.

"Where's your master, dammit? And where's David?"

Joe strolled over to a door in the far wall that she'd assumed led to a closet. Halfheartedly Dany followed and tried the knob. She noted that, unlike the others, this door was constructed of metal. And it was new.

It was also securely locked. "If he's in there, cat, I don't think I can get to him. This isn't the sort of door one kicks in or anything macho like that. Probably leads to his secret laboratory." She pounded on it a few times, to no avail.

As Dany turned away, she passed Max's desk. Out of the corner of her eye she saw a faded manila folder sticking out from under a pile of computer sheets. It struck a chord inside her. It resembled dozens of others she'd seen in the St. Crispin's archives.

She took a closer look. Printed on the tab on the edge of the file was the name RAMBLER, M.

He stole it, Joe. He stole his own file.

She was reaching for it when the metal door swung open with unexpected force. Dany leapt away from the desk as a tall figure emerged from the dark oblong on the other side. She made an involuntary sound that was halfway between a gasp and a scream.

"For God's sake!" Max slammed the door and grabbed her. "Dany? Are you all right? Did the door hit you? Dammit, Dany! I didn't know you were there."

"You startled me, Max." She sagged against him. For a moment all she could think was, thank God, he's not asleep in his coffin, after all.

"What the hell are you doing here?" He pressed her back against the door and leaned close, crowding her. He did not seem particularly glad to see her. "Why are you snooping around inside my house? I told you you weren't allowed in my lab."

"I was looking for you. I wasn't snooping. I just wanted to find you, Max."

"How did you get in?"

"The front door was unlocked. I knocked first. I hammered on the door and yelled your name. You ought to arrange it so you can hear the doorbell down there. It's very annoying not to be able to reach you when I know you're home."

He didn't answer. He just looked at her; the expression in his eyes was cold. As if suddenly remembering it, he shot a quick glance toward the folder on his desk. Dany was glad she hadn't touched it. It looked undisturbed.

Courage, Dany, she told herself. She'd come here to confront him, after all. "I'm also looking for David Ellis. Is he here?"

Max's expression grew even more forbidding. "Why? Has someone bitten his neck again?"

"He's disappeared. He had an appointment last night at midnight." She paused a moment before adding, "Here. With you."

Again Max didn't respond, except by the flicker in his eyes. She'd seen that look once before, on the night they'd met. He was angry.

"Max, we have to talk about David," she said in a more conciliatory tone. "There are a lot of things we have to talk about. There's been too much silence between us. It's no good. I hear things...I suspect things. You've been very evasive with me. I try to trust you, but I'm imaginative and I tend to get carried away with a lot of silly fantasies."

She paused, but he still didn't say anything. More silence between them, silence that ought to be filled with words. She gazed up into his face and felt a moment of disassociation: who is this man? I don't know him; he's a stranger to me.

"You haven't done anything to discourage my suspicions. You won't talk about yourself. How am I supposed to know what manner of man you really are?"

"You could use your intuition," he said coldly. "Or, more pragmatically, you could judge me by my actions, if judge me you must."

"I don't want to judge you. But I've heard some disturbing things about your past, and your present is pretty damn odd, too. You're not normal, Max! You don't have electric lights or a refrigerator. You don't eat. This is the first time I've ever seen you before sunset. We've made passionate love together, and yet I don't know you."

"You've never seen me before sunset," he said harshly.

"What do you—"

"Try looking out the window." He shifted his weight, making her jump. "The sun went down a good ten minutes ago."

"What?" she said stupidly, even as her heart began once again to flutter. A glance through the study window confirmed that the world outside had darkened. Oh my God. Perhaps it was not in the locked upstairs bedroom that the vampire slumbered, but here, behind the iron door.

He leaned into her and raised one hand to her temple. He stroked her hair off her face with the side of his thumb. His expression was fierce, and those hypnotic eyes of his were gleaming. "Nervous, Dany?"

She drew a deep breath. "You love scaring me, don't you?"

He shook his head slightly, twisting that sensual mouth into a frown. "For an intelligent woman, you're pretty damn easy to scare." One of his hands slid down to stroke her throat above the high collar of her blouse. He was gazing at his own fingers on her flesh with that same peculiar fascination she'd noted so many times before.

Dany reached up and tried to push his hands away, but she wasn't strong enough to break his hold. "No," she said. "Don't resort to that again. It's what you always do when I come too close. Zoom in on my superstitions. It's a convenient way, isn't it, to hold me off. Well, it's a tired joke, and I'm sick of it."

"You're still so certain it's a joke?"

She twisted, alarmed to find herself pressed hard against the door. His hands were rough; his mouth was pursed tight. Yes, he was angry. Well, damn him, she had a temper, too.

"Maybe it's not a joke," she retorted. "I've got a bruise on my throat. No, not a bruise exactly. But a mark."

She jerked at the top button of her blouse, but her fingers were too sweat-slippery to open it. "I noticed it after our first night together. It's faded now, but you can still see it, along with several other marks that have shown up since."

"And you're wondering if I've been sucking your blood while you trustingly sleep in my arms? Well, why not? If I were a vampire and you were my human lover I could drink a little from you each night. Not enough to do any real harm. Just enough to get me through the night without being overwhelmed by the urge to kill."

"If? What do you mean, if?" She wrenched herself away from him and tore open the collar of her blouse with both fists. A button popped and rolled away. She bared her throat to him and stood there, her eyes locked with his. "If you're a vampire, *if, if, if,* then prove it. Take me. I offer myself to you. Let's see you commit the ultimate dark act."

"Don't be such a fool. If I'm a vampire, you're inviting your own death."

"Put up or shut up, Rambler. I've had enough of your kinky tricks."

Max slowly folded his arms across his chest. His face was slightly pale, but other than that he revealed no emotion. "So brave, Dany. You just about break my heart."

"Come on, night creature, do it. What are you waiting for? I'm making you this gift of my own free will. Are you afraid to take it?"

He shook his head slowly, still not moving.

"Perhaps you'd prefer to drag me down into the tunnels and rape me? Maybe if you're very vigilant afterward, no-body will ever hear about it."

Max shut his eyes. For an instant—and it only lasted an instant—his face looked so ravaged that Dany wanted to cry. Regret thundered through her. She'd gone too far. What had possessed her to put it that way? She could feel his hurt like an ax blow in her own body.

She reached out and cupped his cheeks in the palms of her hands. "I'm sorry. I didn't mean it. Don't look like that,

Max. I don't even believe it. I came to tell you I don't believe it."

He said one word, a curse, then pulled away from her. He began to pace, his shoulders slumped as if the life had gone out of him.

"Max?" she whispered.

He turned. His eyes met hers for only a second, then dropped. "How did you find out?" He looked once again at the top of his desk. "You read my file?"

"We don't have a file on you. It disappeared."

"I stole it. It's right there on my desk."

"I haven't read it. The head of campus security remembered the story. He told it to me today, when I reported David Ellis missing. Max, listen to me. That was anger talking just now. Anger and frustration. I know you didn't abduct that girl. And I'm absolutely positive you didn't rape her."

He smiled crookedly. "She says I did. You'll always wonder if she was telling the truth. You'll always fear that someday I might turn nasty and do it to you."

"No. I trust you. I'll never think that."

But it was clear that he wasn't convinced. "You've finally got what you wanted," he said bitterly. "Insight into the real me. Max Rambler, rapist. I can't hide from you anymore, can I? Hell, you might as well see the rest."

"What do you mean?"

He stalked past her and wrenched open the metal door. "You want to see me in my true surroundings? You want to know the mysteries that are hidden behind this door? Of course you do; you've wanted it from the start. Okay, Dany, you're going to get your wish. I'm going to take you on a guided tour."

She looked him steadily in the eye. "I trust you, Max," she repeated. "You don't need to show anything to me."

"Don't be so damn noble," he snapped. "You're curious as hell."

She didn't argue as he took her arm and led her through the doorway. A staircase fell away into darkness before them. Max laughed harshly as she hesitated at the top of it. "What's the matter? You feel like Persephone? Don't worry, you're not descending into Hades, nor into the crypt of the vampires, either."

Dany quelled her fears and followed.

There was another metallic door at the bottom of the dark staircase. Max unlocked it with a key, and they walked through into light so bright it was momentarily blinding. Dany put one hand over her eyes. Electric lighting blazed all around them. "This is where I work," said Max.

They were in an enormous underground chamber. The air was dry and cool; she heard the low hum of air conditioners. The walls were a bright lucite-white, and the floor was industrially carpeted. The room was crammed with computer hardware and other high-technology equipment, some of them whirring softly as they ran programs. The ultra-modern ambience of the place put it centuries away from the Gothic mansion and decaying furniture upstairs.

"You see?" Max touched a colored panel and a giant screen lit up on the near wall. She could see the outside of his house, the driveway and the stone steps that led to the front door. "The project is highly secretive, and I have tight security. I ought to have known you had entered the house, but the truth is, I've been sleep-deprived lately because of you, and I was snatching a little nap."

"This is unreal," she said, dazzled by the vast array of technology that surrounded her. "It looks like something from a science-fiction novel."

"I love computers. I love them more than people, most of the time. In fact, I'm trying to design an artificial intelligence system that will have something near to the logical and intuitive capacity of the human brain. A sort of Frankenstein's monster, if you will."

He waved his hands around the cavernous room. "This is the tomb where I spend my days—or my nights, anyway, for it's true that my biological clock is set so I work at night. It's easy for a computer jock to get screwed up that way, since we work in windowless rooms and rarely see the sun."

"Do you work here alone?" she asked, still awed by the glaring luminosity of the place.

"Yes. I enjoy working alone. I left the company I founded because I was tired of being besieged by people's constant demands on my time. I couldn't concentrate, I couldn't create. I'm a loner, Dany. I always have been."

Slowly, she walked around the place. She touched a multicolored power cable coming in from one wall. "You've got electricity to spare."

"Yeah, but I told you the truth when I said the wiring upstairs was old and frayed. These circuits are wired directly to the power source. I don't spend much time in the main part of the house. Fixing the wiring up there is pretty low on my list of priorities. Look."

He opened a door in the right wall and showed her a small cubicle that contained a narrow, unmade bunk, a small refrigerator and a hot plate. She opened the refrigerator. She saw milk, cheese, bread, a jar of peanut butter, some yogurt containers and a couple of six-packs of beer. Food. He was human, after all.

"There's a bathroom with a shower through there," he added, pointing. "I rarely have any need to go upstairs."

Dany sank down on the bunk. Her legs felt weak. She didn't ask why he hadn't shown all this to her before. He must have sensed she wouldn't like it, and he was right. Gloomy and strange though it was, the upper region of the house possessed an Old World mystique that was lacking here. This place, the place he really inhabited, was coldly modern. Sterile. It wasn't a coffin, but in some respects it might as well have been.

"You're disconcerted by this, aren't you?"

He could still read her mind, she noted wryly.

"I think you'd have preferred to be led into a crypt."

"Oh come on, Max—"

"There was a certain romance, a certain appealing danger to the idea of my being a vampire."

"Is that why you kept up the facade? To preserve what you imagined to be my desire for dangerous romance?"

"You enjoyed the fantasy, Dany, don't deny it."

"Yes, but only because I trusted you. Only because deep down I knew I was safe, that it was an act, that you weren't what you were pretending to be."

"But I *am* what I was pretending to be." He made a gesture back toward the computers. "Can't you see? In some odd metaphorical sense, I am a vampire. I'm not normal, as you reminded me. I'm a recluse, antisocial. I get the warmth that I require by latching on to someone now and then and sucking the life out of them until they no longer have anything left to give me. I'm like the moon, glowing with reflected light, without a heat source of my own. My soul's as cold and barren as a rock."

"That's not true!" She saw him with Sarah, down on the living room carpet, laughing as he allowed her to climb all over him. She saw him with her, pushing up on his elbows to see her face while he loved her, his hands, his lips, his eyes radiating pleasure. "If you seriously believe that, you're a fool."

"And Livvie Kenworthy? Was she a fool, too?"

"She was a liar," Dany said.

He laughed without mirth. "Tender, trusting Dany. What makes you so sure I didn't rape her?"

"You couldn't do such a thing."

"No? Maybe you're the fool."

Ignoring this, Dany held out her hand. "Sit down beside me. Tell me about her. I want to hear your side."

He shook his head. She saw he wasn't going to yield, oh no, not one iota. "That's my bed," he said. "That's where I toss and turn and fantasize about making love to you. If I join you there it won't be for a chat."

She set her chin. "Just come here."

"Damn you!" Eyes blazing, he came. With all his considerable strength, he pushed her down beneath him and covered her body with his own. He took her lips, punishing them. He forced her lips open with the rough pressure of his tongue.

Dany didn't fight him. She could feel the tension shooting through him, making his movements stiff, his entire body tense as a board. And yet with every bitter word, with every kiss, she understood him better. He had been hurt. Deeply. His vaunted shyness was something of another order: an insecurity, a lack of confidence in both himself and other people. He was lashing out at her to protect himself. He didn't know yet that he didn't need to, that all she wanted was to shelter him and make that hurt go away.

You love him.

She didn't know where the thought had come from, nor why it had struck her at this moment. It was as if a voice inside her was speaking, a voice that was far wiser than she. Love him, trust him. He needs that from you. He needs it to make him whole.

She obeyed the voice and yielded to the driving pressure of his body, surrendering everything that he in his fury might have been tempted to plunder. She wrapped him in her arms. When they were close like this, nothing else seemed to matter. Any antipathy between them vanished as if it had never existed.

At length Max dragged his mouth from hers and lifted his head. His eyes were dreamy, but as she looked into them they cleared, turning ice-hard once again. "If we could make love twenty-four hours a day, there'd be no problem, would there?"

"Perhaps there's less of a problem than you think." She shifted so they were lying on their sides, facing each other. "Talk to me, my darling. It's time. I've taken a lot of risks with you. Even when I was afraid, I didn't turn away. It's your turn now to trust me, to take that chance."

A haunting pain clouded his features. "Hell, Dany. It's been years since anyone's penetrated my defenses the way you do." He rested his head on his palm, avoiding her gaze. "I never meant to get so tangled up with you. Emotionally, I mean. I thought I could just have the sex—take it and run. But instead I want to *be* with you. And I've been terrified you'd find out about my past. Dammit, Dany. I can't even contemplate what it would feel like to lose you now."

"You're not going to lose me. But you have to talk to me, Max. You have to open up."

He closed his eyes, and sighed, and did.

Eleven

―――

If I haven't told you about my youth, it's partly because it's not something I care to remember," Max said. "My father drank, my mother repressed her feelings and encouraged me to do the same. We had lots of money but no joy in one another. I escaped into my fantasies, and later into the exciting new wonders of computer technology. I wasn't very good at relating to my peer group, so I didn't have many friends. The few kids I did pal around with were like me—shy, bright dreamers who invented worlds to live in that were more tolerable than this one."

Lying beside him, her head pressed to his shoulder, Dany lightly stroked his chest, full of compassion for the lonely boy he must have been. She knew the type well—kids on the fringes, separated from their peers by the very characteristics that often made them successful a few years down the line—intelligence, originality, creativity, combined with an I'll-show-them mentality. The years of being on the outside looking in were usually short for such people, but that didn't make the experience any less painful.

"I'd been playing various games down in the tunnels for about a year at this time, just myself and a couple of other kids. We'd go down there and pretend to be fighting demons, something we couldn't do in our prosaic real lives. There was a sense of adventure in it, too, as you can attest yourself after being down there. It can be dangerous, and there's a physical challenge involved. I was no good at football, baseball, basketball, all the traditional sports that boys are supposed to excel at in high school, but I took up fencing and karate to fight my imaginary monsters, and I grew to be an expert at navigating the tunnels."

"Was Olivia Kenworthy one of the kids who played down there with you?"

"No, but in other respects Livvie was a lot like me. Shy, awkward, socially a loner. She was good at math, and we got to be friends. She was smart and also very pretty, although she seemed to have no awareness of her own appeal. She dressed in the most ghastly clothes, and never wore makeup, so she always looked kind of rumpled. But I didn't care about that."

"Were you in love with her?"

"Yes. That powerful, sweeping, damn-the-consequences kind of love you feel when you're eighteen and still a little afraid of girls. Oh yes," he added as she shook her head skeptically, "I was a nervous wreck about it, believe me. My only salvation lay in the fact that poor Livvie was even more frightened then I.

"I got up my nerve and called her a few times, making up various excuses, like needing the chemistry assignment. At length, I got really brave and asked her out. But she wasn't allowed to date. Her mother was ridiculously strict. I tried to talk her into sneaking out with me, but Livvie was afraid of her mother, who enforced discipline with a leather belt. The woman had terrorized her all her life.''

Dany's hands clenched into fists. "Barbarian."

"Yeah," he said grimly. "Livvie had it rough. Anyway, I was a bright kid, remember, very good at problem-solving. I figured out a way to be with her. If Livvie couldn't come out to me, I'd go in to her. And that proved easy, given the fact that she lived with her mother in the headmistress's cottage."

Dany blinked. "My house? Of course. I'd forgotten for a moment that she must have lived there. But what's so special about the headmistress's cottage?"

Max pushed himself up on his elbow. "To go any further in this tale I'm going to have to let you in on one of my little secrets."

She ran a finger over his lips. "Well? Which one, mystery man?"

He nipped her gently. "How I walk through walls."

"Another supernatural talent bites the dust, huh? Okay, let's have it."

"I'm surprised it hasn't occurred to you already. I believe I explained to you that all the campus buildings were connected by the tunnel system. The headmistress's cottage is officially part of the St. Crispin's campus."

"You mean there's an entrance to the tunnels in my house?"

"Yup. There's a closet in your basement that you've apparently never examined too closely. I've been in and out of there several times during the past few days."

After a moment of stunned silence, Dany began to laugh. Playfully, she pummeled his stomach. "You devil. All this time I thought that if you weren't a vampire, you must surely be a housebreaker. I kept checking my locks, wondering why there was never any sign of anything being jimmied or forced."

"I'm going to put a lock on that closet door for you, Dany. If I can get in, someone else might be able to, too."

She nodded, feeling a little nervous at the idea of Jennifer alone in the house taking care of Sarah. Jennifer was David's girlfriend and David knew his way around the tunnels. History repeating itself.

"So you sneaked into Livvie's bedroom while her whip-wielding mother was asleep?"

"I'm afraid so. We were full of rioting hormones that gradually overcame the shyness plaguing us. We made love. But instead of giving us ease, this intimacy only increased our torment. We couldn't be seen together. We were terrified of getting caught, and to make matters worse, the school year was ending and a separation was looming ahead of us. I'd been accepted to MIT, but Livvie was going to Cal Tech, three thousand miles away. We were desperate. We couldn't see beyond the moment. The only solution seemed to be to get married. We'd both been lonely all our lives and all we wanted was to be together. But Edith Kenworthy wouldn't allow it."

"You went to her for permission?"

"In retrospect it seems a stupid thing to do. We'd been so damn careful that until then, the ogre had been completely in the dark. We should have left her that way, but I thought telling her was the honorable thing to do. She had a fit. She forbade Livvie to see me again and grounded her." He laughed shortly. "Little did the headmistress know that I already had access to her house."

"You don't have to tell me the rest," Dany said gently. "It's obvious what happened. You decided to run away together, but you didn't get far. You ended up hiding out in the tunnels, and they found you."

"That's right. In the meantime, clever old Edith was claiming her daughter had been kidnapped. She manufactured a ransom note and gave it to the police. She ripped a leaf out of one of my notebooks and used one of my pens. The forensic abilities of the Chesterton police proved equal to the task of deciding it was me, particularly since I'd gone missing at the same time Livvie had.

"They found us, and Livvie panicked. God only knows what her mother did to her to make her say those things about me." Dany could hear a vestige of the pain he must have felt at being accused of rape by the girl he'd loved. "Used the belt, I suppose."

"You were never charged, were you?"

"My parents were wealthy, and old Edith was eager to settle out of court. No doubt she feared Livvie might turn around and tell the truth. She sent Livvie off to the West Coast as fast as possible, and I never heard from her again. I learned later she got married a few months afterwards— found another guy pretty fast." His voice hardened. "I hated her for a while. I felt betrayed, as you can imagine. It's never been easy for me to trust people, and this made it almost impossible. It certainly embittered me on the subject of romantic love."

"But you were young, Max. There's no reason to remain bitter forever."

"You've seen how I live. Over the years, I've withdrawn from people more and more. I'm a loner, and that's the way I like it. I'm not going to change."

"But you have changed. You don't hate Livvie anymore, do you?"

"No," he said slowly. "She was seventeen and scared. I have compassion for her now, but, believe me, my current attitude has taken a number of years to evolve."

"I'm not sure I could ever forgive something like that."

"It hasn't been easy, but I've tried."

"The fact that you've tried is one of the things I love about you, Max."

He stiffened. She could feel his sudden emotional withdrawal. "Don't say that, Dany. Haven't you been listening? I explain why I've got a stone in my chest instead of a heart, and you tell me you love me?"

"Yes. I love you." Dany leaned over and unfastened the top three buttons of his shirt. She pressed her lips to the warm, bare flesh and murmured, "Stones don't beat. They don't leap about when the flesh covering them is caressed."

He sucked in his breath and wound one hand into the hair at the back of her neck. "I think you ought to go now, Dany."

She laughed.

"I mean it. You'd better get out while you can. If you come any closer, you'll be hurt; you'll be emptied just as surely as if I'd sunk my teeth into your veins and sucked you dry."

"I don't believe you." She had the shirt entirely unbuttoned now. She pushed it off his shoulders, then ran her palms over the feast of flesh there exposed. "And I'm not afraid. I love you, Max. I love you."

"No, Dany. Don't keep saying that!"

"Why not? Why not, if it's true?"

"If?" he repeated, the corners of his mouth turning up. *"If, if, if?"* His hands slid up her arms to her shoulders. She could feel them trembling. "You know what I want, don't you? It's not love, it's an obsession. If you're not out of here in ten seconds I'm going to rip off your clothes and bury myself inside you."

In answer she lowered his hands to her own buttons. "Come on then, tough guy. Do it. Make love to me."

He made an agonized sound in the back of his throat. She was reckless, he thought. Crazy. "Aren't you a little leery about opening your body to an alleged rapist? You've bought my story, apparently, but I could have made it all up.

You don't *know*, Dany. There's no way for you to ever be sure."

"I recognize the truth when I hear it."

She undid her buttons herself and tossed her blouse onto the floor. Her bra quickly followed. Max groaned at the sight of her naked breasts, all pink and ivory, the peaks already erect. This is it, he thought. She's gone too far. There were limits to his self-control.

But deep inside him, a bewildered joy was building. She'd heard his story and believed it. She'd seen his life-style and accepted it. He'd played upon her superstitious fancies for days, half expecting to drive her away, but she was not afraid.

Dany stroked his hair as Max reached overhead and flicked a switch that doused the lights, then with a quick shift of their bodies he was on her, his hard, lean form pressing her down, his blood beating in erotic rhythm with hers. He kissed her once, then raised his head until his sulky mouth was hovering over hers. "You had your chance to escape." He rotated his hips, letting her feel his intense arousal. "Now it's too late."

She struggled a little, taking pleasure in the raw power he used to restrain her. Desire was knifing through her belly; she tossed her head frantically as he pinned her wrists together on the pillow over her head. He straddled her waist-high and explored her breasts with his other hand while she arched against him, still trying—but not very hard—to free herself. "You like it pirate-style?" he whispered. "A little subtle domination on my part?"

"My deepest, darkest fantasies come true." She stopped fighting and allowed her body to go slack beneath his. He felt good. He felt wonderful. "No, scratch that. I guess my deepest, darkest fantasies have to do with vampires."

"No vampire could possibly do all the things I'm going to do with you." He released her hands and brought them up to touch the warm flesh over his racing heart. "Vampires are cold, dead. Vampires don't ache to spill their life force into the warm body of their lover." For an instant his eyes took on a merry glint. "How could you possibly still worry about vampires after making love with me?"

"My dear man, I've never sat down and studied the anatomical abilities of vampires! And you did put a mark on my throat, after all."

"Ah, but you have such a pretty throat, Dany." He fastened his mouth upon it and bit her gently. "I couldn't resist sucking it, just a little."

She moaned as his hands caressed her bare breasts. She tugged at his waistband, wanting him naked, wanting him hard between her thighs. "Plus, you didn't eat my ice cream. You gave it to the cat."

"You saw that?" He reared up and shrugged off the open shirt. "And I tried so hard to conceal it from you. I'm allergic to chocolate. If you'd brought vanilla or rum raisin, I'd have devoured the entire carton."

"I don't know, Max. I still think there's something strange about you."

"Wait till you hear *my* deepest, darkest fantasies." Kneeling over her, he opened his belt and unzipped his jeans. Smiling, she reached out and touched him through the open zipper. She had the pleasure of hearing him groan. It took him a second to catch his breath before saying, "Oh baby, you're so good to me. I want to give you the sweetest, wildest, most passionate experience of your life."

"I love you, Max," she said, folding her arms around his waist. There was a kind of awe in her voice as she repeated, "I really love you."

"Poor Dany." He kicked off his jeans and pushed her skirt up around her waist. "You love a creature of darkness. The only saving grace is that maybe, just maybe, he's beginning to love you, too."

She smiled. "Can't you say it a little more definitely than that?"

"Don't press your luck. That's the closest I've come in seventeen years. Now hush."

He pressed his mouth to hers and kissed her ferociously until they were both beyond speech.

Later, much later, Dany stared up at the ceiling and said, "I'd love to stay here with you, my darling, but I've got to organize a search for David Ellis."

Max shifted. "Don't worry about David. I know where he is."

"But you told me you hadn't seen him!"

"I haven't. But I did get a message from him. I found it this morning, slipped under my front door."

So that was why David had written down the directions to Max's house. He had been here, although not at her lover's request.

"The note contained a challenge," Max went on. "A Dominance Duel, as it's called in the game. I'm supposed to meet him tonight in the tunnel under the soccer field and do battle. The winner is acknowledged to be the Ancient One."

"Oh my God."

"It's a direct challenge to my authority. He really does see me as the Ancient One, it seems. He's out to dethrone me."

"Terrific."

"So you see, David hasn't disappeared any more than I did all those years ago. He's down in the tunnels, waiting for me."

"He's Olivia Kenworthy's son, Max."

"Yes, I know. I realized it as soon as you told me his mother's name. Ellis was the name of the guy she married. It makes sense now, doesn't it? Why he's been after me."

"A kind of sense, I suppose."

"He wants revenge. At his age, I'd have probably felt the same if I'd thought someone had kidnapped my mother and raped her."

"Are you going to go?"

"Yes. It's time to end this, don't you think? What I'm wondering is, should I let him win the duel, or does he need an authority figure to beat the dickens out of him for once in his life? The kid's a terror. I'd sure as hell like to knock a little sense into him."

"That's all we need," she said dryly. "I'm coming with you."

"No. I know you don't like the tunnels. I don't want to drag you down there again."

Her voice was stubborn. "I insist."

He rolled over and smiled. "Which of us are you planning to protect?"

"Neither. I'm going to referee. I'm not having any macho Dominance Duels on my campus, Max. If you've got something to settle with David, you and he can do it with words."

"That would be okay with me, love, but I don't think words'll reach the boy at this point. But the game might."

"So far I think the game's caused nothing but trouble."

He shook his head. "You say you trust me. Trust me in this."

"Are you sure you know what you're doing?"

"Is anyone ever sure? No, I suppose not. But I remember what it's like to be David's age. He's a bit like I was, I suspect. He needs someone to set him straight, and it might as well be me."

"You won't hurt him?"

Max rolled over and pressed her body down beneath his, treating her once again to the erotic caress of his hard chest and belly against her tender skin. "What do you think?" he whispered.

Whatever breath she might have had left to answer with was stolen away by his kiss.

Twelve

———

Dany and Max entered the tunnels later that evening through the closet in Dany's basement. They were both dressed in jeans, sweatshirts and sneakers, standard tunnel gear, according to Max. She wore no makeup this time, and she was carrying two extra flashlights and a rough map of the tunnels that Cass had unearthed from the archives. Jennifer was babysitting. Dany had given her special permission to stay out after curfew, even to sleep at the headmistress's house if necessary. Max wasn't sure how late they were going to be out.

"If I know the way this kid's mind works," he said, "he's not going to make it easy for us to find him."

He proved right in this assumption. When they got to the reasonably wide and civilized tunnel that Max said was the designated meeting place, there was no sign of the boy. What they found instead, balanced on a wide steam pipe, was a cassette tape recorder. Max pressed play, and they heard David's voice saying, "Welcome to the crypts of the vampires. You have begun your quest."

"Welcome? He's got to be kidding." Dany was already hot from the steam waves in the tunnels—it was a sticky, jungle heat. Max had told her that the temperature in the tunnels varied according to where they were—in some areas it was humid, in others desert-dry. There were even some cold spots where the temperature would suddenly drop twenty or thirty degrees. "You don't dare dress too lightly, despite the heat," he'd explained, "You never know when you might hit a frigid zone."

"I don't understand how anyone could find these tunnels fun," she said now.

"It's the challenge that's fun, love." She could tell from his voice that he was already getting into it.

David's tape continued, "To join in the game, you must assume the role of one of the creatures of the night. I am a master vampire. What will you be?"

Dany looked around warily. "I'll bet he's hiding in an alcove somewhere, waiting to see what we answer."

"I, too, am a master vampire," Max intoned. "My companion is human, a magic adept."

"What's that?" she whispered.

"A sorceress."

"I think I'd rather be a vampire, since everybody else is. I'd just as soon not have to worry about somebody sneaking up and tearing my throat."

"Your throat will be fine. You've got strong magic against vampires. Come on, there's an archway to the left that will take us deeper into the maze."

"Great. I can't wait."

The dark was like a cloak around them, thick and impenetrable; even their flashlights seemed to do little to dispel it. Worse, as they moved down the low, narrow passageway Max had chosen, their nostrils were assaulted by an unpleasant odor, something that reminded Dany of rotten fish. "It's probably the mold on the walls," Max said. He played his light along the wall to their left. "See that green slime? It really stinks."

"I feel like being sick."

"Come now, Dany, you're a sorceress, remember? Make a potion to ward off nasty smells."

"And you're a master vampire, with senses that are even more acute than mine. Why aren't you reeling?"

"I also have a superhuman will that allows me to ignore my sensory input if necessary. That's one of my strengths."

They came to what appeared to be a dead end. "Okay, partner," he said, "wave your ivory staff to find a secret opening."

Dany waved her flashlight instead, and dimly, in a corner to their right, she saw a flash of color high up on the wall. They approached and looked more closely. In Gothic lettering someone had painted This Way to Middle-Earth.

"So here we are in Tolkien's world. But which way? I still don't see any way out of here."

Beside her Max had dropped to his knees. "Look. Yeah, I remember this." He was pointing to a pipeline opening in the wall that was perhaps twenty inches in diameter. "It leads to a secret chamber."

"You're not telling me we have to crawl through that?"

"'Fraid so."

"Max, I love you, but this is ridiculous. For all we know he didn't even come this way."

"I think he did. The paint looks fresh, and I'm betting he's chosen a complicated quest for us."

"How do you know the tunnel isn't booby-trapped?" Dany had a frightening vision of the various forms David Ellis's revenge might take. He's just a troubled kid, she told herself. Up to mischief, yes, but not dangerous. Surely not.

"I don't think he means to hurt us, Dany. That's not his game, nor is it the way of Hunt the Night City. The purpose is to frighten, yes, but the danger exists in the player's imagination, not in reality."

"With all due respect for the benignity of your game, we're not at my dining room table tonight. We're in a real maze, with real dangers, and we're essentially at the mercy of someone who believes you guilty of a real crime."

"Which is why I didn't want you along on this adventure, Dany. If there is any danger, I'd prefer to encounter it alone. You stay here. I'll continue on and come back before long with a report."

Dany made a face. She was blasted if she was going to let him do that. She had the feeling that a calm female presence might be needed to mediate between the two males. "No. I'm coming." She knelt down beside him. "I've got my magic spells in working order, and I'm ready to venture."

The crawl through the pipelike tunnel was about as bad as it could be. The heat was more intense inside, and the smell was positively sulphurous. "I think I've died and gone to hell," Dany muttered as a blast of hot steam erupted just behind her. The floor of the passageway was slimy against her palms, and she was just as happy not to look at whatever was growing on the walls. She had a fantasy about a bubble bath, clean and sweet-smelling....

"Aha," said Max. He was ahead of her.

"What?"

"End of tunnel, beginning of relief."

Sure enough, within a couple of yards they emerged into a large chamber that was dimly lit by a bare light bulb hanging from a fraying cord on the ceiling. The air was much cooler. Dany looked around, blinking as her eyes adjusted to the light. She could see an oblong item against one wall. Another coffin? "Where are we?"

Max stood up and approached the object. It was a wooden mock-up of a rack, complete with wheel and ropes. It was quite authentic-looking. "The prop room of the drama club again," she commented.

"Nice work," said Max, touching it. "I'm half inclined to believe this sucker really works. How do you suppose he got it in here?"

"No doubt it comes apart."

Behind the rack metal manacles had been hammered into the wall. "This is obviously the torture chamber. Nothing like getting the details right," Max said dryly just as the overhead light went out.

Dany let out a small yelp of surprise. Max's hand immediately reached out to squeeze hers. "I'm fine," she said, trying to ignore the way her knees were shaking. Don't get an attack of the superstitious vapors now, she ordered herself. You're contending with a teenager, not a monster. She snapped her flashlight on again. "Power failure?" she asked calmly enough.

"More likely a little elf has turned off the lights. David?" he yelled. "Come on out. Let's not drag this out all night."

Silence.

"Is there another way out of here?" Dany asked. "I'd just as soon not crawl through that pipe again."

By the beam of his flashlight Max studied the map. "If we're in the area I think we're in—and this map is by no means completely accurate, by the way—there should be a grille over there in the left-hand corner."

Dany wasted no time in checking. "Yes. I've found it." She tugged. "It seems to be stuck. Guess my spells aren't working."

"Let's try mine." Max came over and applied brute force to the grille. He managed to wrench it off, disclosing an opening that was a good four feet high this time. Compared to the pipe they'd just crawled through, this one seemed positively mammoth.

As he put down the grille, Dany felt something small and furry scramble over her foot. "Ugh. Did you see that?"

"Yeah. A rat."

She shuddered. "For God's sakes, let's get out of here."

She was just stepping through the grill when her flashlight caught something—no, someone—moving up ahead. "Look, Max, there he is! David? Stop!"

"Follow," the boy's voice intoned as he disappeared around a bend.

"You're supposed to be fighting a duel, not running away," she retorted.

David paid no attention. They pursued, moving into a larger, colder passageway. "I mean it, Ellis," Dany shouted. "I've had about enough of this. I've got a child waiting for me at home. Max and I aren't going to play this silly game any longer."

They came to a place where the tunnel widened and the ceiling overhead rose. Max grabbed Dany's wrist and jerked her to a stop. "Wait," he whispered near her ear. "He's here, I sense it. Don't move."

They were blinded as the beam of a floodlight suddenly stabbed the darkness. David Ellis's voice said, "Go home and leave him to me, Ms. Holland. You weren't supposed to be here anyway."

Dany stared into the light, willing her eyes to adjust. "Well, I am here, David. I'm here to make sure you and Max come to some sort of mutual understanding."

The boy gave a harsh laugh that reminded her of Max at his most bitter. "More likely we'll come to blows."

Max's fingers found and touched her lips for silence. "I've accepted your challenge, David," he said. "I'm ready to fight the Dominance Duel. But first I want to know the reason you've been persecuting me."

"You're a fine one to talk about persecution, considering what you did to my mother."

"What did I do to your mother? I want to hear it from your lips."

"You raped her." The boy flung the words at him. "Here, in the tunnels. Look around you, Rambler." The blinding light abruptly turned away from their eyes and Dany could finally see that they were in another chamber. It was fairly large, about twelve feet square. "Don't you recognize the place where you held her prisoner for three days?"

Max didn't look at their surroundings; instead, his attention was focused on David, who stood tensely on the far side of the room. Dany noted similarities in the way both males were standing—legs slightly apart, arms loose at their sides. Then she noticed something else. David had a long, slender object in his right hand. She blinked, realizing it was a fencing saber.

At his last school, David had been on the fencing team. Her brain whirled. She realized she hadn't asked Max exactly what a Dominance Duel consisted of. In her experience with Hunt the Night City, duels were decided on the basis of several throws of the dice.

"I recognize the place, yes," said Max. "But you weren't even born then, David. Who told you about your mother and me? Was it Livvie herself who accused me?"

"She knows nothing. It was my grandmother who told me what sort of man you really are. She told me before she died, and I'm grateful to her. I'm grateful because otherwise I might have come to you not knowing. How humiliating that would have been!"

"Why?" Max persisted. His voice was low, encouraging. "Why would you have come to me at all?"

"I don't have to explain myself to you!" David cried. He advanced several steps toward them. "I brought another saber. Let's get on with it."

"You expect me to fence with you?"

"Obviously. It's a duel, after all."

"I'm a computer genius, not a jock," said Max calmly. "I don't know how to fence."

He was lying, Dany knew. He did know how to fence. It had been one of the few sports he'd been good at; he'd told her so. Too good, perhaps. He didn't want to humiliate the boy, she sensed.

"Then I guess you'll lose, won't you? Don't worry, you won't die." David's voice was contemptuous. "The tips are blunted."

"Nobody is going to fight a real duel, blunted tips or no blunted tips, on my campus," Dany said severely. "Throw the blasted dice—I presume you both have loaded sets so the winner will obviously be the cleverest cheat—and be done with this nonsense."

They paid no attention. They had closed upon each other, and were standing only a yard apart. There was something very similar about them. David was blond and Max was dark, but the set of their shoulders, the slender, almost elegant line of their bodies was almost identical.

No sooner had she noted this when everything suddenly tumbled into place. "Dear God," she whispered to no one in particular. She remembered the photograph of David that had been clipped to his St. Crispin's application. There had been something odd about it, something that had caught her attention and tantalized her. The eyes. They weren't green, but the shape, the setting, the arching eyebrows—they were Max's eyes.

Was it possible? Had Olivia become pregnant as a result of her relationship with Max? Was that the reason she'd married so soon after being separated from him? Dany made a quick calculation. David was sixteen, and the ill-fated love affair had taken place approximately seventeen years ago. It fit, of course it fit.

They were father and son.

"You challenged me, David," Max was saying. "That means I choose the weapon."

For the first time, the boy looked uncertain.

"Throw down the sword. Simple hand-to-hand combat is what it's going to be."

David didn't move, nor did he obey. Max was taller than he was and, presumably, stronger.

"I'm holding you to the rules of honor," Max added. "As a devoted player of the game, you know I have that right."

"Fine! Have it your own way." Defiantly, David threw down his weapon. "I don't care how we do it as long as I get my hands on you."

"Max," Dany said.

He spared her a brief glance. "Don't interfere, Dany. Please."

He's your son, she wanted to shout. She thought of Sarah, having nightmares because she'd been abandoned by her father. At least she'd had a father. *I might have come to you not knowing.* Had David sought out his natural father, only to hear from his still-vindictive grandmother that he'd been conceived in violence? Was he fighting to avenge his mother, or to console himself for the years without a father's love?

Oh, God, it was so ironic! Max loved kids; he loved Sarah. How he'd have treasured this boy; how different his life would have been. They'd both been cheated. Now, when they should have embraced and forgiven each other, they were squared off to do battle.

David took up a wary stance, both fists aggressively raised. Max followed suit. They circled for several moments, then Max moved in with a sharp right jab that glanced off the boy's upraised wrist. David's return punch connected, knocking Max backward.

"Damn," he muttered. "The kid can box."

Everything happened very quickly after that. Max came roaring back with a quick combination that drove David against one of the walls. The boy retorted with a quick blow in Max's stomach that made him groan.

"Stop it, both of you!" Dany cried. They were going to hurt each other, damn them. There was real violence zinging the air between them. "He didn't rape your mother, David; they were in love. Your grandmother was a vicious liar. Stop it!" she added as another punch landed on Max's jaw.

They ignored her, and it quickly became apparent that Max was getting the worst of things. It was not because he lacked skill, however. More than once he refused to take advantage of a perfect opening. Without being too obvious about it, he was letting David win.

David clipped him hard in the ribs, and Max staggered and nearly fell. Dany had all she could do to stop herself from throwing herself between them. Neither would appreciate the interruption, she knew.

"You bastard," David muttered, landing another solid punch. "I've dreamed of this."

"Cocky damn kid, aren't you?" said his father. He surprised everybody by letting out a bloodcurdling yell and striking out with the side of one hand on David's neck. The boy dropped to his knees, weaving for a moment before he regained his balance. "Not fair," he gasped. "That was karate."

"I said hand-to-hand combat. I didn't specify which type." He jerked David's head back so he was forced to look at him. "Do you yield?"

David shook his head, struggling to his feet. Max waited until he was steady, then hit him again.

"Max!" Dany screamed.

"That was for Dany," he said. "For dragging her into something that should have been kept between you and me, for making her life miserable these last couple of weeks."

Once again, David was attempting to regain his feet. "Oh, so you protect your women, do you, Rambler?" he said bitterly. "Well, I pity her, getting mixed up with you."

"I try to protect the woman I love, yes. Just as I would have loved and protected my children, if I'd ever been aware that I had any."

He knows. Dany felt her tense limbs relax. Until this moment she'd had no idea whether or not Max had put it all together. He hadn't known before tonight, she was certain of that.

David raised his head and met his adversary's eyes. "It's true then, isn't it?"

"That I'm your father? Yes, David, apparently it's true. Although this is a helluva way for me to find out."

"You knew! You've known for years!"

"I didn't know until ten minutes ago," Max countered. "If I had, you can bet I'd have made sure you didn't grow up to be such a hurt and angry teenager."

There was a moment of electric silence as they stared at each other. Then Max got a grip on David's arms and helped him to his feet. "I loved your mother," he said quietly. "I didn't kidnap or rape her, and it's my guess that she'll admit it if you ask her. If I'd known of your existence, I'd have followed her out to the West Coast and married her, no matter what your grandmother had to say about it. But I didn't know. She never told me she was pregnant." His voice rose in pitch and intensity. "She never told me I had a son."

"I don't believe you," David cried. "You're a smooth-tongued liar. You raped her and you abandoned me, and I'll never forgive you for that as long as I live!"

As if to emphasize this, David knotted his fist and drove it into his father's undefended jaw. Max's eyes rolled. To Dany's horror, he swayed and crumpled to the floor.

Thirteen

You'll help me with him, David," Dany said. "You'll help me get him home or by God you'll be expelled from St. Crispin's so fast you won't know what hit you."

"He'll be all right," David said grudgingly. "He's starting to come around already. I know a shortcut that leads back toward your house." He was standing to one side while Dany cradled Max's head in her lap. Her lover's face was bruised, and one of his lips was bleeding copiously.

"You'll carry him if you have to, damn you." Dany was more angry than she could ever remember feeling in her life. "He's your father and he loves you, foolish idiot that you are."

David stared at her sullenly. "He's never cared two pins about me for the entire sixteen years of my life."

"He never knew you existed. He loves children. He's been like a father to Sarah from the moment he met her. He drove hours through a snowstorm one night when she was sick to help me get her to a doctor. He's a wonderful man, and you've made one hell of a mistake.''

"My grandmother told me—"

"Your grandmother lied. What happened between your mother and Max was no different from what's happening between you and Jennifer Stokes—young love, first love, the kind of love your grandmother hated and would have had your liver on a platter for.''

David looked miserably embarrassed. "How do you know about Jenny and me?"

"You'd be surprised, the things I know. Bend down here and help me.''

With his assistance she roused Max, who seemed only half-conscious as they dragged him to his feet.

"Lean on your son's shoulders,'' she ordered. "He's going to help me get you back to my house.''

"I can walk,'' Max said unsteadily.

"Do as I say, both of you,'' Dany snapped. "My God, you look more like a vampire than ever,'' she added, wiping blood off his mouth with her sleeve.

Max managed a laugh. "C'mere. A little taste of your throat will revive me faster than anything else.''

David blinked. "He's not really a vampire,'' he said to Dany. "You didn't believe that, did you? The bruise on my throat was stage makeup. I just said that to get you curious about him. To call your attention to what he was, and what he'd done.''

"Why?'' Max asked. "Why should it matter to you that Dany know about my past?''

"I wanted everyone at St. Crispin's to know. You got off scot-free. When I went to hear your robotics lecture last spring everybody thought you were terrific. I wanted them to know the truth.''

"Only one person can tell you the truth, David. I suggest you have a talk with your mother before you throw any more punches my way." He paused. "By the way, you've got one hell of a right jab, kid. My compliments."

The mutinous look on the boy's face softened slightly, and it occurred to Dany that there might be some hope of a reconciliation, after all.

When Max tried to walk he got dizzy, and Dany insisted that David support him on the slow hike back through the tunnels to the headmistress's house. "Help get him up to the living room sofa," she insisted when they gained her basement.

Jennifer was delighted to see David. "Oh, thank goodness you're okay. I've been so worried! Why didn't you tell me you were going down there?" She looked back and forth between him and Max. "What happened? What did you do to each other?"

"They fought," said Dany.

"And I lost," said Max cheerfully. He stretched out on Dany's sofa, deliberately exaggerating the weakness he felt. His jaw was aching, it was true, and the journey back to Dany's through the tunnels had been excruciating, but even so, he didn't feel too bad. He couldn't take his eyes off David. His son. It was an extraordinary thing. All these years, he'd had a son. If only he'd known. He felt like strangling Olivia for never telling him.

"You would have won," David admitted, "if I hadn't turned around and hit you when you weren't expecting it."

Max patted the sofa beside him. "Sit down a minute, David." He looked beyond him to Dany and Jennifer. "Will you leave us alone for a bit?"

Dany nodded and urged the girl out of the room. David retreated, as if to follow them, but Max reached out and got a grip on his wrist. "Stay. You owe me a hearing, at least."

"Why should I believe your paltry explanations?"

"I wasn't going to offer any explanations. I was going to ask you to tell me about your life."

"What do you mean?"

"You're my son and I don't know you." Max suddenly understood how Dany must have felt when he'd so deliberately kept her in ignorance about his past. How had she put up with it? "I want to know you, David, your favorite things to do, your dreams, your plans. The things you're scared of, the things that make you angry, the things you love. All that stuff. Talk to me."

The wistful look that crossed the teenager's face told Max something right away. As did the cynicism with which he said, "I don't believe you. You don't really care. You're just trying to disarm me."

"Why would I bother to disarm you? Why not just tell you to leave, to get the hell out of my life, if that's what I really wanted?"

"I'm sure that's exactly what you *will* tell me, sooner or later. You're weird. A loner. You don't care about anybody or anything, except your damn robots. I know all about you, Rambler. You have no human contacts. It was easy to convince people you were a vampire because you certainly don't act like an ordinary man."

Max had the curious sensation of seeing his own words, his own actions come back to hit him in the face. The very arguments he'd used to defend himself against his growing attachment to Dany were now being used against him by this boy, this child, this miraculous creation of his own life force.

David had raised a telling point. How could he possibly convince him that the way he had lived for so many years was no longer the way he wanted to live? That something had changed, changed through Dany's agency? That because of her, Max wasn't the same person he'd been twenty-four hours before.

The thought of his cold, sterile laboratory repelled him now, as did the memory of those night hikes through the forest for exercise with only his cat for company. The idea of living alone for the rest of his life, without love, without a family, chilled him to his core. In David, in this lonely, defiant boy, Max saw himself, his past. And in the Max Rambler of twenty-four hours ago he saw the desolate outcast David might someday turn out to be.

He could prevent that. It wasn't too late for David. Thanks to Dany, it wasn't even too late for *him*. But how, how to make the kid see?

He tried, he tried hard. Doggedly, he introduced one subject after another, desperate to hit upon something to which David would respond. But he got nowhere. It wasn't like charming Sarah, who, despite her father's desertion, was far too affectionate a child to ever turn away from love. Sarah, after all, had a generous, warmhearted, uninhibited mother to give her confidence and open her to intimacy. David had had Livvie, who'd been so scared of life she'd betrayed the one person who might have helped her break the tyranny of her mother. However much she might have matured and changed in the past seventeen years, Livvie had obviously been unable to provide David with the emotional security he'd needed.

Maybe it *was* too late.

Max was still wracking his brain for a way to reach his son when they were interrupted by a voice in the doorway that led out to the front hall. "Mommy?" Sarah whispered. Her face was sleep-heavy, and tears were sticking to her lashes. "I can't find my mommy, Max."

Max instinctively sat up, holding out his arms for Sarah. "She's around somewhere. I'll find her for you. In the meantime, come here, love."

Sarah ran to his side. Ignoring his aching head, he hauled her into his lap and cuddled her. "I had a bad dream," she said, pressing her face against his chest.

"Shh, sweetheart, it's okay." Max rocked her back and forth. She was trembling, poor kid. "There's nothing to be afraid of Sarah. Your mommy's in the kitchen, I guess, and I'm right here." He gently kissed the top of her head and felt her tense little body slowly begin to relax. "Go back to sleep, sweetie. You're safe; I've got you."

"I love you, Max," the child whispered.

"I love you, too."

As the child's eyes drifted shut, Max glanced over toward his silent son. He was shocked to see moisture glistening on the boy's cheeks.

"David?" Dammit! He wanted to comfort the kid, but he didn't know how.

"She's not your daughter," he said bitterly. "You've only known her for a couple of weeks, and she's no relation to you."

"True," said Max evenly. "But I love her anyway." As he spoke the words, he knew he meant them. He loved Sarah, and he loved her mother even more.

David jerked to his feet and turned his back. "You weren't there for me when I woke up from a bad dream."

"No. But I'm here now," said Max. He waited a moment, then added, "And I'd like to love you too, Son, if you'll let me. I'd like to try and make up for all those lost years."

David's shoulders slumped, and he brushed one hand over his eyes. Max felt the tension in his own limbs; he was wound up tight, he realized, with the fear that his new-found child would reject him, storm out of the room, leave and never come back.

But David surprised him and, probably, himself as well. He didn't leave.

Dany left them alone for as long as she could, talking to Jennifer, trying to explain what had happened. At length she prevailed upon the tired girl to go upstairs and sleep in the spare bedroom. After getting her settled, she went in to check on Sarah. Her heart nearly stopped. Sarah was not in her bed.

Every horrible fantasy she'd ever had about the disasters that might happen to her child raged in full color through her brain. She ran to check the bathroom. No Sarah. Had she awakened from a nightmare, wandered downstairs and somehow gotten out of the house? An even more chilling possibility occurred to her: what if Sarah had gone down to the basement, found the open closet that led into the tunnel system, and wandered into that dark, hellish maze?

Terrified, Dany flew down the stairs to the living room. "Max!" she cried. "I can't find Sarah. I—" She stopped on the threshold. Her daughter was lying in Max's arms, fast asleep. And David was sitting beside them on the sofa, Sarah's bare feet in his lap, earnestly talking to his father about computers, robots and artificial intelligence.

Wordlessly, Dany crossed to them and lifted Sarah into her own arms to take her back to bed. "She had a bad dream," Max explained.

"It's awfully late," she said in a neutral tone. "Is anybody besides myself thinking of going to bed?"

Max glanced at his watch. "Hell, Dany, it's only two-thirty. I don't get tired this early." He glanced at David. "You tired, kid?"

"Me? No," David said. "I stay up late and sleep during the day."

Dany raised her eyes to heaven. "Don't tell me I've now got *two* vampires on my hands."

"Face it, Dany," said Max. "Your destiny lies with us creatures of the night."

She could hear them both laughing as she carried Sarah upstairs.

Max didn't join her in bed that night. A scant five hours later, when Sarah rose for the day, bright and lively, with no apparent memory of her bad dreams of the night before,

Dany took her downstairs for breakfast. She heard no sound from the living room. Had Max and David left the house to continue getting acquainted elsewhere? Maybe they'd gone back to his place.

"Mommy, come and look," Sarah whispered from the archway that led into the living room. "It's the funniest thing."

Dany joined her daughter on the threshold. They were there, both of them, sound asleep, the man on the sofa and the boy stretched out on the floor. Dany smiled as for the first time ever she saw the light of the rising sun caressing Max Rambler's slightly bruised, but very human face.

"The first thing I'm going to do is have the circuits re-wired in this place," said Dany early in the new year when her husband carried her over the threshold of his spooky Gothic house.

"And destroy the atmosphere? How could you possibly contemplate such a thing?"

"Then I'm going to buy a refrigerator. A proper-sized one suitable for our large—and growing—family."

Max lovingly patted her stomach. He was fiercely proud of the new life that was already developing within her. The new baby had been conceived on their honeymoon, much to the delight of both parents.

Dany covered his hand with hers and smiled archly. "Do you realize how easily you've changed from a reclusive bachelor to a loving husband and father who enjoys inti-macy?"

"You sure worked a miracle on me."

He took her up to the room at the end of the hall that had once been locked against her. Even before the wedding, Dany had already gone to work on the room, tossing out the massive furniture in favor of something a little more con-temporary, pulling down the heavy drapes to let in the light.

Her makeup was all over the master bathroom now, her clothes in Max's closets, her shoes on the floor. There was a new Stephen King novel on the bedside table, although Dany hadn't found the opportunity to begin reading it yet. Max had other ideas about the way her time should be spent in bed.

"We're going to have to tell Sarah and David about the baby soon," she said as they undressed for the night. "Sarah will be thrilled, I'm sure. She'd been asking for a new brother or sister for years. But I'm not sure about David. Do you think he'll be upset?"

"Jealous, you mean? No, I don't think so. He's adjusted to the entire situation pretty well."

It was true. David was still living in his dorm at St. Crispin's, but he often spent the weekends with them. He'd talked to his mother, who had apparently been horrified to learn that her son had heard and believed his grandmother's malice. Livvie had fully exonerated Max, and told David the true story. She'd even called Max to beg his forgiveness for the lies she'd told so many years before.

"He'll be surprised, though, I'll bet," Max added with a grin. "No doubt it'll come as a shock to him that anyone over the advanced age of thirty is still capable of having sex."

Dany giggled. "Practically all we ever *do* is have sex!"

"Nonsense," said Max, stripping off his last garment and getting into bed beside her. She went eagerly into his arms, never tiring of the feel of that long, graceful body against her own. "We do other things. We talk, for instance, and work, and play with Sarah, and you're teaching me to cook."

"Don't forget our mammoth sessions of Hunt the Night City. You've really got me hooked on that."

"Yeah, and you've been beating the dickens out of me," he groused. "David and I were saying just last night that if

you keep winning so often, we're going to have to acknowl-
edge *you* as the Ancient One." He slid down in bed and
nuzzled her belly, then began teasingly kissing her breasts.
"Maybe I should challenge you to a Dominance Duel," he
said huskily. "We could fight it right here in bed."

"No fair. You'd trounce me."

"Yeah?" He reared up on his hands and knees and settled her beneath him. "Why?"

"You have a secret weapon, one that I just can't seem to
resist." She reached out a finger and pressed it to his delicious, carnal mouth. "This. When you put it to my throat,
I very willingly go down to defeat."

"Don't tempt me." He lowered his body to hers and
sought that tender, vulnerable spot on her throat with his
tongue. "Mmm," he added as she squirmed a little beneath him. "You've got a fetish about this, don't you?
That's okay; so do I."

"We're perfect for each other, you know that? I love you,
Max."

Dany waited a second, then opened her eyes. He was
grinning, but silent. Stubborn devil.

"Well?" she prodded.

"Okay, okay, I admit it: I love you, too," he told her, and
proceeded to demonstrate how much.

"Max?" Dany whispered a little while later.

"Mmm?" His voice was thick.

"Are you falling asleep?"

He perked up immediately. "Who, me?"

"You are!" she crowed. "Your precious biological clock
is slowly adjusting to mine."

"Bull," he said.

"It is! Soon you'll be getting up with the sun and sleeping at night like a normal person."

"No chance, lady."

"Well, you're going to have to get up early tomorrow," she went on. "At seven a.m., to be precise. School vacation's over, and you promised to get breakfast for Sarah and put her on the bus."

He groaned loudly. "The joys of fatherhood, huh? I knew there had to be a catch to this intimacy routine."

"Will you do it? You *did* promise, and I have an early meeting with the trustees."

"I'll do it," he said resignedly. "This must be love," he added as he reached over and set the alarm clock.

Dany caressed his hair and kissed him. "Greater love hath no vampire than he who would venture out in the early-morning sun to see his little girl off to school."

Max smiled and pulled her close. "There's no such thing as vampires, Dany," he reminded her.

"I know, I know, but Max, I've been thinking...this house is so old and creepy, and once or twice I've heard the oddest sounds in the middle of the night. Do you suppose we have ghosts? You *do* believe in ghosts, don't you? I mean, it is perfectly possible that someone's spirit could remain attracted to the place where he or she had lived, and return now and then to visit—"

"Don't start, Dany, don't start." Her husband was laughing at her. "I only know one way to put a stop to these outlandish superstitions of yours."

So saying, he kissed her into silence.

*...and now an exciting short story
from Silhouette Books.*

*

HEATHER GRAHAM POZZESSERE

Shadows on the Nile

CHAPTER ONE

Alex could tell that the woman was very nervous. Her fingers were wound tightly about the arm rests, and she had been staring straight ahead since the flight began. Who was she? Why was she flying alone? Why to Egypt? She was a small woman, fine-boned, with classical features and porcelain skin. Her hair was golden blond, and she had blue-gray eyes that were slightly tilted at the corners, giving her a sensual and exotic appeal.

And she smelled divine. He had been sitting there, glancing through the flight magazine, and her scent had reached him, filling him like something rushing through his bloodstream, and before he had looked at her he had known that she would be beautiful.

John was frowning at him. His gaze clearly said that this was not the time for Alex to become interested in a woman. Alex lowered his head, grinning. Nuts to John. He was the one who had made the reservations so late that there was already another passenger between them in their row. Alex couldn't have remained silent anyway; he was certain that he could ease the flight for her. Besides, he had to know her name, had to see if her eyes would turn silver when she smiled. Even though he should, he couldn't ignore her.

"Alex," John said warningly.

Maybe John was wrong, Alex thought. Maybe this was precisely the right time for him to get involved. A woman would be the perfect shield, in case anyone was interested in his business in Cairo.

The two men should have been sitting next to each other, Jillian decided. She didn't know why she had wound up sandwiched between the two of them, but she couldn't do a thing about it. Frankly, she was far too nervous to do much of anything.

"It's really not so bad," a voice said sympathetically. It came from her right. It was the younger of the two men, the one next to the window. "How about a drink? That might help."

Jillian took a deep, steadying breath, then managed to answer. "Yes ... please. Thank you."

His fingers curled over hers. Long, very strong fingers, nicely tanned. She had noticed him when she had taken her seat—he was difficult not to notice. There was an arresting quality about him. He had a certain look: high-powered, confident, self-reliant. He was medium tall and medium built, with shoulders that nicely filled out his suit jacket, dark brown eyes, and sandy hair that seemed to defy any effort at combing it. And he had a wonderful voice, deep and compelling. It broke through her fear and actually soothed her. Or perhaps it was the warmth of his hand over hers that did it.

"Your first trip to Egypt?" he asked. She managed a brief nod, but was saved from having to comment when the stewardess came by. Her companion ordered her a white wine, then began to converse with her quite normally, as if unaware that her fear of flying had nearly rendered her speechless. He asked her what she did for a living, and she heard herself tell him that she was a music teacher at a junior college. He responded easily to everything she said, his voice warm and concerned each time he asked another question. She didn't think; she simply answered him, because flying had become easier the moment he touched her. She even told him that she was a widow, that her husband had been killed in a car accident four years ago, and that she was here now to fulfill a long-held dream, because she had always longed to see the pyramids, the Nile and all the ancient wonders Egypt held.

She had loved her husband, Alex thought, watching as pain briefly darkened her eyes. Her voice held a thread of sadness when she mentioned her husband's name. Out of nowhere, he wondered how it would feel to be loved by such a woman.

Alex noticed that even John was listening, commenting on things now and then. How interesting, Alex thought, looking across at his friend and associate.

The stewardess came with the wine. Alex took it for her, chatting casually with the woman as he paid. Charmer, Jillian thought ruefully. She flushed, realizing that it was his charm that had led her to tell him so much about her life.

Her fingers trembled when she took the wineglass. "I'm sorry," she murmured. "I don't really like to fly."

Alex—he had introduced himself as Alex, but without telling her his last name—laughed and said that was the understatement of the year. He pointed out the window to the clear blue sky—an omen of good things to come, he said—then assured her that the airline had an excellent safety record. His friend, the older man with the haggard, world-weary face, eventually introduced himself as John. He joked and tried to reassure her, too, and eventually their efforts paid off. Once she felt a little calmer, she offered to move, so they could converse without her in the way.

Alex tightened his fingers around hers, and she felt the startling warmth in his eyes. His gaze was appreciative and sensual, without being insulting. She felt a rush of sweet heat swirl within her, and she realized with surprise that it was excitement, that she was enjoying his company the way a woman enjoyed the company of a man who attracted her. She had thought she would never feel that way again.

"I wouldn't move for all the gold in ancient Egypt," he said with a grin, "and I doubt that John would, either." He touched her cheek. "I might lose track of you, and I don't even know your name."

"Jillian," she said, meeting his eyes. "Jillian Jacoby."

He repeated her name softly, as if to commit it to memory, then went on to talk about Cairo, the pyramids at Giza, the Valley of the Kings, and the beauty of the nights when the sun set over the desert in a riot of blazing red.

And then the plane was landing. To her amazement, the flight had ended. Once she was on solid ground again, Jillian realized that Alex knew all sorts of things about her, while she didn't know a thing about him or John—not even their full names.

They went through customs together. Jillian was immediately fascinated, in love with the colorful atmosphere of Cairo, and not at all dismayed by the waiting and the bureaucracy. When they finally reached the street she fell head over heels in love with the exotic land. The heat shimmered in the air, and taxi drivers in long burnooses lined up for fares. She could hear the soft singsong of their language, and she was thrilled to realize that the dream she had harbored for so long was finally coming true.

She didn't realize that two men had followed them from the airport to the street. Alex, however, did. He saw the men behind him, and his jaw tightened as he nodded to John to stay put and hurried after Jillian.

"Where are you staying?" he asked her.

"The Hilton," she told him, pleased at his interest. Maybe her dream was going to turn out to have some unexpected aspects.

He whistled for a taxi. Then, as the driver opened the door, Jillian looked up to find Alex staring at her. She felt . . . something. A fleeting magic raced along her spine, as if she knew what he was about to do. Knew, and should have protested, but couldn't.

Alex slipped his arm around her. One hand fell to her waist, the other cupped her nape, and he kissed her. His mouth was hot, his touch firm, persuasive. She was filled with heat; she trembled . . . and then she broke away at last, staring at him, the look in her eyes more eloquent than any words. Confused, she turned away and stepped into the taxi. As soon as she was seated she turned to stare after him, but he was already gone, a part of the crowd.

She touched her lips as the taxi sped toward the heart of the city. She shouldn't have allowed the kiss; she barely knew him. But she couldn't forget him.

She was still thinking about him when she reached the Hilton. She checked in quickly, but she was too late to acquire a guide for the day. The manager suggested that she stop by the Kahil bazaar, not far from the hotel. She dropped her bags in her room, then took another taxi to the bazaar. Once again she was enchanted. She loved everything: the noise, the people, the donkey carts that blocked the narrow streets, the shops with their beaded entryways and beautiful wares in silver and stone, copper and brass. Old men smoking water pipes sat on mats drinking tea, while younger men shouted out their wares from stalls and doorways. Jillian began walking slowly, trying to take it all in. She was occasionally jostled, but she kept her hand on her purse and sidestepped quickly. She was just congratulating herself on her competence when she was suddenly dragged into an alley by two Arabs swaddled in burnooses.

"What—" she gasped, but then her voice suddenly fled. The alley was empty and shadowed, and night was coming. One man had a scar on his cheek, and held a long, curved knife; the other carried a switchblade.

"Where is it?" the first demanded.

"Where is what?" she asked frantically.

The one with the scar compressed his lips grimly. He set his knife against her cheek, then stroked the flat side down to her throat. She could feel the deadly coolness of the steel blade.

"Where is it? Tell me now!"

Her knees were trembling, and she tried to find the breath to speak. Suddenly she noticed a shadow emerging from the darkness behind her attackers. She gasped, stunned, as the man drew nearer. It was Alex.

Alex . . . silent, stealthy, his features taut and grim. Her heart seemed to stop. Had he come to her rescue? Or was he allied with her attackers, there to threaten, even destroy, her?

* * * * *

Watch for Chapter Two of SHADOWS ON THE NILE coming next month—only in Silhouette Intimate Moments.

ATTRACTIVE, SPACE SAVING BOOK RACK

Display your most prized novels on this handsome and sturdy book rack. The hand-rubbed walnut finish will blend into your library decor with quiet elegance, providing a practical organizer for your favorite hard-or soft-covered books.

Only $9.95

Approximately 16" x 8" when assembled

Assembles in seconds!

To order, rush your name, address and zip code, along with a check or money order for $10.70* ($9.95 plus 75¢ postage and handling) payable to *Silhouette Books*.

Silhouette Books
Book Rack Offer
901 Fuhrmann Blvd.
P.O. Box 1396
Buffalo, NY 14269-1396

Offer not available in Canada.

BKR-2A

*New York and Iowa residents add appropriate sales tax.

 ## Silhouette Desire

COMING
NEXT MONTH

#385 LADY BE GOOD—Jennifer Greene
To Clay, Liz was a lady in the true sense of the word, but she wanted
more from him than adoration from afar—she wanted him to be this
particular lady's man.

#386 PURE CHEMISTRY—Naomi Horton
Chemist Jill Benedict had no intention of ever seeing newsman
Hunter Kincaid again. Hunter was bent on tracking her down and
convincing her that they were an explosive combination.

#387 IN YOUR WILDEST DREAMS—Mary Alice Kirk
Caroline Forrester met Greg Lawton over an argument about a high
school sex ed course. It didn't take long for them to learn that they
had a thing or two to teach each other—about love!

#388 DOUBLE SOLITAIRE—Sara Chance
One look at Leigh Mason told Joshua Dancer that she was the woman
for him. She might have been stubbornly nursing a broken heart, but
Josh knew he'd win her love—hands down.

#389 A PRINCE OF A GUY—Kathleen Korbel
Down-to-earth Casey Phillips was a dead ringer for Princess
Cassandra of Moritania. Dashing Prince Eric von Lieberhaven
convinced her to impersonate the kidnapped heiress to the throne, but
could she convince him he was her king of hearts?

#390 FALCON'S FLIGHT—Joan Hohl
Both Leslie Fairfield and Flint Falcon were gamblers at heart—but
together they found that the stakes were higher than either had
expected when the payoff was love. Featuring characters you've met
in Joan Hohl's acclaimed trilogy for Desire.

AVAILABLE NOW

In response
to last year's outstanding success,
Silhouette Brings You:

Silhouette Christmas Stories 1987

Specially chosen for you in a delightful volume celebrating the holiday season, four original romantic stories written by four of your favorite Silhouette authors.

Dixie Browning—*Henry the Ninth*
Ginna Gray—*Season of Miracles*
Linda Howard—*Bluebird Winter*
Diana Palmer—*The Humbug Man*

Each of these bestselling authors will enchant you with their unforgettable stories, exuding the magic of Christmas and the wonder of falling in love.

A heartwarming Christmas gift during the holiday season...indulge yourself and give this book to a special friend!

Available November 1987 XM87-1